ELEGIES

ALBIUS TIBULLUS was born between 55 and 49 BC. He wrote two books of elegies, the first, addressed to Delia, was published in 27 or 26 BC, the second, addressed to Nemesis, appeared shortly before his death in 19 or 18 BC. His patron was the aristocrat M. Valerius Messalla Corvinus. Tibullus set out in his patron's entourage on a mission to the East in 30–29 BC, but fell ill in Corcyra and returned home to Rome (Elegy 1.3). He probably accompanied Messalla on his campaign in Gaul against the Aquitanians (28–27 BC), for which his patron was granted a triumph in 27 BC (Elegy 1.7) and during which Tibullus was granted military honours. Tibullus was of equestrian rank (a Roman knight) and probably quite wealthy despite his protestations of poverty. He possessed a villa at Pedum, between Tibur and Praeneste. He was good-looking and took pride in his appearance. He died young at around the age of thirty and was survived by a mother and a sister.

A. M. JUSTER is a poet and translator. His books include *Longing for Laura* (2001), *The Secret Language of Women* (2003), winner of the Richard Wilbur Award, and Horace's *Satires* (2008). He has won the Howard Nemerov Sonnet Award three times.

ROBERT MALTBY is Emeritus Professor of Latin Philology at the University of Leeds. His books include *Latin Love Elegy* (1980), *Tibullus, Elegies: Text, Introduction and Commentary* (2002), and *Introduction to Latin* (2011).

T0054920

OXFORD WORLD'S CLASSICS

*For over 100 years Oxford World's Classics have brought
readers closer to the world's great literature. Now with over 700
titles—from the 4,000-year-old myths of Mesopotamia to the
twentieth century's greatest novels—the series makes available
lesser-known as well as celebrated writing.*

*The pocket-sized hardbacks of the early years contained
introductions by Virginia Woolf, T. S. Eliot, Graham Greene,
and other literary figures which enriched the experience of reading.
Today the series is recognized for its fine scholarship and
reliability in texts that span world literature, drama and poetry,
religion, philosophy, and politics. Each edition includes perceptive
commentary and essential background information to meet the
changing needs of readers.*

OXFORD WORLD'S CLASSICS

TIBULLUS

Elegies

Translated by
A. M. JUSTER

With an Introduction and Notes by
ROBERT MALTBY

OXFORD
UNIVERSITY PRESS

OXFORD
UNIVERSITY PRESS

Great Clarendon Street, Oxford OX2 6DP

Oxford University Press is a department of the University of Oxford.
It furthers the University's objective of excellence in research, scholarship,
and education by publishing worldwide in

Oxford New York

Auckland Cape Town Dar es Salaam Hong Kong Karachi
Kuala Lumpur Madrid Melbourne Mexico City Nairobi
New Delhi Shanghai Taipei Toronto

With offices in

Argentina Austria Brazil Chile Czech Republic France Greece
Guatemala Hungary Italy Japan Poland Portugal Singapore
South Korea Switzerland Thailand Turkey Ukraine Vietnam

Oxford is a registered trade mark of Oxford University Press
in the UK and in certain other countries

Published in the United States
by Oxford University Press Inc., New York

Translation © A. M. Juster 2012
Latin text, editorial material © Robert Maltby 2012

First published as an Oxford World's Classics paperback 2012
Reprinted with corrections 2013

The moral rights of the author have been asserted
Database right Oxford University Press (maker)

All rights reserved. No part of this publication may be reproduced,
stored in a retrieval system, or transmitted, in any form or by any means,
without the prior permission in writing of Oxford University Press,
or as expressly permitted by law, or under terms agreed with the appropriate
reprographics rights organization. Enquiries concerning reproduction
outside the scope of the above should be sent to the Rights Department,
Oxford University Press, at the address above

You must not circulate this book in any other binding or cover
and you must impose this same condition on any acquirer

British Library Cataloguing in Publication Data

Data available

Library of Congress Cataloging in Publication Data

Library of Ciongress Control Number: 2011934718

Typeset by RefineCatch Limited, Bungay, Suffolk
Printed in Great Britain
on acid-free paper by
Clays Ltd, Elcograf S.p.A.

ISBN 978-0-19-960331-2

11

CONTENTS

ACKNOWLEDGEMENTS

For pp. vii–xi and xvi–xxiii of the Introduction, and for the 'Note on the Text' (p. xxvii), Professor Maltby has drawn on parts of the Introduction of his *Tibullus: Elegies. Text, Introduction and Commentary* (Francis Cairns: Cambridge, 2002), presenting the material in an abridged form. The Explanatory Notes, likewise, are extracted from his Commentary in that volume, to which interested readers should turn for fuller information and for references to secondary sources.

Pages xxiii–xxv are abridged from R. Maltby, 'The Unity of *Corpus Tibullianum* Book 3: some stylistic and metrical considerations', *Papers of the Langford Latin Seminar* 14, eds F. Cairns and M. Griffin (Francis Cairns: Cambridge, 2010) 319–40.

The Latin text, 'A Chronology of Tibullus', and 'Textual Notes', are based on the Latin text, 'Chronological Guide', and 'Textual Note' respectively of A.G. Lee, *Tibullus: Elegies*, 3rd edition, revised in collaboration with Robert Maltby (Francis Cairns: Leeds, 1990). The Latin text has been altered at the following places: 1.2.90; 1.3.4, 13; 1.4.44; 1.5.42, 60; 1.10.11, 70; 2.2.21; 2.3.53, 65; 2.5.68, 81.

INTRODUCTION

TIBULLUS was one of three great Roman elegists whose work has come down to us. His love poems addressed to Delia and Nemesis vie with the elegies of his contemporaries Propertius and Ovid as some of the finest of the classical period. He lived in a violent period of transition between the end of the Republic and the beginning of the Empire; a period which witnessed the assassination of Julius Caesar, and the civil wars culminating in the defeat of Antony by Octavian at Actium. It was a high point of Roman literary culture, where the poetry of Virgil and Horace and the prose works of the historian Livy and the polymath Varro alongside the works of the elegists attested to a Golden Age of Latin literature.

The Life and Works of Tibullus

Information about Tibullus' life is scarce. Apart from the poems themselves, which as a mixture of fact and fiction must be used with care, and brief mentions in contemporary poets, there are two short pieces of biographical evidence attached to most of the manuscripts which transmit his poems. The first is an epigram on his death, attributed to his contemporary, the Augustan poet Domitius Marsus:

> Unfair death, sent you also, Tibullus, in your youth
> As Virgil's comrade to the Elysian fields,
> So there should be no one to sing soft loves in elegiacs
> Or of royal wars in heroic metre.

The second is a brief *Life*, a short prose biography, probably derived from Suetonius' lost work on the lives of the poets, dating to the end of the first century AD:

Albius Tibullus, a Roman knight, noted for his good looks and remarkable for his personal adornment, above others loved the orator Corvinus Messalla, as whose aide in the Aquitanian War he was awarded military decorations. In the opinion of many he occupies first place amongst the writers of elegy. Also his amatory epistles, although short, are extremely subtle. He died a young man, as the epigram above shows.

Virgil died in September 19 BC, so Tibullus' death must have been around the same time, perhaps late 19 or early 18 BC. There is no direct evidence for his date of birth, but both the epigram and the life agree that he died young, and the consensus among scholars is that he was born between 55 and 49 BC. Ovid lists the Roman elegists in the order Gallus, Tibullus, Propertius, and Ovid. Gallus was born in about 69 BC and Propertius between 54 and 47 BC, whereas Ovid himself was born in 43 BC.[1] Ovid also informs us that Tibullus was survived by his mother and sister.[2] His father is never mentioned and the fact that Tibullus depicts himself as in charge of his family estate (1.1, 1.10, 2.1) makes it likely that he was dead by the time Tibullus reached manhood.

The latest datable event mentioned in Tibullus' first book of elegies is the triumph of Messalla over Aquitania, which can be dated on inscriptional evidence to 25 September 27 BC. This would place the publication of the first book in 27 or 26 BC, shortly after the publication of Propertius' first book of elegies in 28 BC, but before the completion of Propertius' second book in 24 BC. Tibullus' second book refers in Elegy 2.5 to the installation of Messalla's son, Messallinus, to a priesthood in about 19 BC, shortly before Tibullus' death. There is some uncertainty about whether the second book was published by the author or posthumously.

Tibullus' *praenomen* is given as Albius in the *Life* and in two poems addressed by Horace to a poet named Albius who is almost certainly Tibullus.[3] This Albius is said by Horace to have been born in Pedum, in the region of Latium near Rome.[4] If this is true it would make Tibullus one of the few truly Latin poets, as opposed to Horace and Ovid, who were Italians, and Catullus and Virgil, who were provincials.

Tibullus claims that his once prosperous family estate had recently been reduced in size (1.1.19–22, 33, 41–2). Possibly his estate, like those of Horace and Propertius, had suffered in Octavian's land-confiscations of 41–40 BC, undertaken to provide land for his veterans after the battle of Philippi. Other explanations are possible. There were later land-confiscations in 36 and 31 BC.

---

[1] *Tristia* 2.445–68 and 4.10.51–4.
[2] *Amores* 3.9.49–52, an elegy on the death of Tibullus.
[3] Horace, *Odes* 1.33, *Epistles* 1.4.   [4] Horace, *Epistles* 1.4.2.

Alternatively, an Albius referred to by Horace as having a mania for collecting bronzes, which led to a reduction in his family fortune, could have been Tibullus' father.[5] One must be careful, however, not to take Tibullus' references to his own 'poverty' (1.1.5, 1.5.61–5) too seriously. The motif of the poet's 'poverty' is conventional in Hellenistic and Augustan poetry and tells us nothing about the poet's actual finances. Rather it is a relative term, with positive moral overtones, implying modest means rather than actual poverty. Horace calls him rich[6] and in the *Life* he is described as a Roman knight, for which the minimum property qualification was 400,000 sesterces, a considerable sum in modern terms. There can be no doubt that Tibullus was a member of the cultivated, literary Roman elite.

Tibullus' patron, mentioned both in the *Life* and in the poems themselves, was the aristocratic soldier, statesman, and man of letters Marcus Valerius Messalla Corvinus (64 BC to AD 8). Messalla is named in the opening poems of both Tibullus' books of elegies (1.1.53, 2.1.31 and 33), which are thus dedicated to him as patron. His literary circle in Rome, which included his niece, Sulpicia, author of [Tib.] 3.13–18, and the young Ovid, was second only to that of Maecenas, patron of Horace, Virgil, and Propertius. Messalla himself was a noted orator, and a stickler for purity in Latin style, who dabbled in philosophical and grammatical studies and composed pastoral and erotic verse in Greek. Tibullus' famed elegance of diction could have owed something to his patron's refined and learned literary tastes.

Elegies 1.3, 1.7, and the *Life* make it clear that Tibullus' duties to his patron included military service. Elegy 1.3 refers to Tibullus' illness in Corcyra, while accompanying Messalla on a mission to the East and to Egypt. Elegy 1.7 mentions Tibullus' involvement in Messalla's campaign in Aquitania (lines 9–12), for which his patron was granted a triumph in September 27 BC. The dating of the campaigns mentioned by Tibullus in Elegies 1.3 and 1.7 is uncertain, but it is likely that Messalla went first to the East in 30–29 BC before becoming governor of Gaul in 28–27 BC, where he conquered the Aquitani. He spent much of the spoils of victory on public works in

---

[5] Horace, *Satires* 1.4.28.   [6] Horace, *Odes* 1.33.7.

Rome and on the repair of the Via Latina, mentioned in 1.7.57–62. In 26–25 BC he resigned his office as City Prefect as being incompatible with his republican ideals, but there was no break with Augustus. In 20 BC he was appointed to the distinguished priestly college of the Arval Brothers and in 19 BC his son, Messallinus, was elected to the same college, an event recalled in Tibullus' most ambitious poem, 2.5. Messalla, then, was a strong ally of Augustus. He was joint consul with him in 31 BC and was involved at the highest level in imperial military and domestic policy, including Augustus' religious and moral revival. These concerns are reflected in the works of his protégé Tibullus.

In many ways Tibullus can be seen to be more in tune with the ideology of the new Augustan regime than his fellow elegists. After the end of the civil wars Augustus saw it as his task to renew traditional values and religious practices. He built or restored numerous temples in the city of Rome and passed moral legislation encouraging traditional marriage amongst Roman citizens. Tibullus' often expressed preference for the moral simplicity of an earlier agricultural age (as in 1.3 and 2.1), his interest in traditional Roman religion (as in 1.1.and 2.1), and his positive attitude, when it suits his purpose, towards marriage and family life (as in 2.2 and 1.7), as well as his support for his patron in the performance of his military and civil duties (1.1, 1.7), are all consonant with the propaganda, if not the practice, of the new regime. The image of personified Peace with which the first book ends (1.10) relies heavily on official iconography connected with the end of the civil wars. The themes of 2.5 with its religious setting and its excursus on the foundation of Rome, reflecting ideas in Virgil's national epic, the *Aeneid*, is in tune with the preoccupations of the Augustan regime in the run up to the Saecular Games of 17 BC, which neither Virgil nor Tibullus lived to see.

Against this can be set the fact that Tibullus never mentions Octavian/Augustus by name, omits any mention of Octavian's victory at Actium, even in Elegy 2.5, and fails to include in his discussion of Messalla's career in 1.7 his patron's joint consulship with Octavian in 31 BC. The positive attitude to Egypt and its religion demonstrated in 1.7 also runs counter to official propaganda in which Egyptian religion was portrayed in an extremely unfavourable light after the fall of Antony (31 BC), who had used Egypt as his base. In this Tibullus differs from his fellow poets, Virgil and Propertius, both of whom reflected official opposition to Egypt.[7] Elegy 1.7 was written in the year of Gallus' disgrace and recall from Egypt (27 BC) and mentions an embassy by Messalla to the East and Egypt (1.7.13–22). It could be that Messalla had shown some independence in attempting to rehabilitate Egypt and its culture after the defeat of Antony and that Tibullus was showing his support for this position.[8] In fact most of the apparent anti-Augustan elements discussed in this paragraph could be put down to Tibullus' single-minded loyalty to his patron rather than to a thorough-going opposition to the current regime, with which, as we have seen, he was for the most part in sympathy. Tibullus may share at a literary level the anti-war stance which is characteristic of the elegiac view of the world to be found in Propertius and Ovid, but his poems for Messalla (1.7) and his son, Messallinus (2.5), show a mature acceptance that the peace of the Roman Empire depended on the active involvement of her citizens in war and other civic duties. As an elegist Tibullus had to be in favour of love outside marriage and in opposition to war, but underlying this literary stance is the voice of a moral traditionalist, a loyal supporter of his aristocratic patron, whose views largely coincided with the spirit of the new Augustan age.

Tibullus and Elegy

Tibullus, along with Gallus (whose works are now lost), Propertius, and Ovid, belongs to a group of poets known as the Latin elegists, all writing in the second half of the first century BC. Elegy, in the broad sense of poetry written in the elegiac couplet (hexameter followed by pentameter), has a long history in classical Greek and Roman poetry, stretching back in Greece as far as the seventh century BC. It could be connected etymologically with the Armenian word *elegn*, 'flute', referring to poetry originally sung to a flute accompaniment, but ancient grammarians considered it meant 'a song of lamentation' derived from the Greek *e e legein*, 'to cry woe, woe!' The elegiac

---

[7] Virgil, *Aeneid* 8.698–700, Propertius 3.11.41.
[8] See introductory note to 1.7.

couplet was considered appropriate for the expression of direct and immediate concerns, as opposed to hexameter, which was the metre for continuous narrative, such as Homer's epics. It was used in the early Greek period for a variety of topics, usually hortatory in style and addressed to a particular person or group. Subjects included military exhortation, mythological narrative, moralizing meditations, and political diatribe. By the late fifth century it became associated in particular with lamentation. At the end of this century it died out, possibly because prose took over as a more appropriate medium for much of its subject matter. It comes to life again in third-century Alexandria, where it took on two distinct forms: mythological narrative, giving a serious treatment of the loves and emotions of mythological heroes and heroines, and short amatory epigrams, often purporting to deal with the author's own affairs in a witty and detached manner. Both these types influenced the Roman elegists, but whereas Greek amatory epigram had been rather light in tone, the Romans applied to their own feelings and amatory affairs the seriousness which their Greek predecessors had reserved for mythological tales. In giving a more developed and serious treatment to his own experiences the Roman elegist would often take as his starting point a traditional theme from Greek epigram. The opening of Tibullus 1.2 provides a good example of this, taking its inspiration from an epigram of Meleager.[9] Mythological themes from narrative elegy could then be used to illustrate the elegist's own predicament. This use of mythology was more characteristic of the elegies of Propertius and Ovid than of Tibullus, but the myth of Apollo and Admetus in Tibullus 2.3[10] provides a developed example of this technique.

   The development of elegy in Rome begins in around 100 BC when a group of aristocrats, including Q. Lutatius Catulus, Valerius Aedituus and Porcius Licinius, had begun to dabble in the composition of Latin erotic epigrams in elegiac metre on the Alexandrian Greek model. They may have been inspired by the publication around this time of a collection of earlier Greek epigrams known as the 'Garland' of Meleager. Meleager was a Greek poet active around 100 BC. His own epigrams were usually on erotic subjects, addressed

---

[9] See note to 1.2.1.   [10] See note to 2.3.11.

to both boys and girls. In his 'Garland' he collected together epigrams by Greek poets of the previous two centuries, alternating the authors and linking the poems thematically. The Roman epigrammatists inspired by these works were full-time politicians with only an amateur interest in poetry. In the next generation changing social and political conditions gave rise to a new type of poet, referred to disparagingly by Cicero as 'the neoterics' or 'new poets'. These were aristocrats of independent means who could devote themselves almost full time to poetry. They wrote for themselves and their friends and could experiment with new forms, often again inspired by Alexandrian Greek models. A key figure in spreading these Greek literary ideas in Rome was the Greek poet and literary critic Parthenius, who had been taken by the Romans as a prisoner of war and freed in Italy in 73 BC. He influenced the new Roman poets of the sixties and fifties BC, the best known of whom, for the modern audience, and the only one whose work has survived intact, is Catullus.

Catullus experimented with various types of narrative mythological elegy, with short, mixed-metre lyrics on personal topics, and with epigrams in the elegiac metre. It is in the cycle of lyric and elegiac poems concerned with his feelings for a certain Lesbia (probably in real life the aristocratic Clodia) that Catullus lays the foundation for Augustan love elegy. Both in the literature and in the plastic arts of this period in Rome there was a greater interest in the individual, a feature often stressed as more characteristic of the Roman than of the Greek artistic sensibility. Taking his framework from Greek amatory epigram, Catullus was able to change its tone from light and ironical to the serious and analytical. In the complex elegiac poem 68B Catullus uses mythology to illustrate and deepen his own personal feelings of love for Lesbia and sorrow at the death of his brother. In 68A the addressee, Catullus' love-sick friend Allius, becomes the prototype for later elegiac lovers, unable to sleep, unable to take pleasure in poetry, and likened to a shipwrecked sailor on the point of death. These are all images that will appear later in Tibullus and his fellow elegists in their descriptions of their own sufferings. Many of the situations and attitudes typical of later elegy can be seen in the works of Catullus, but its potential as a genre had yet to be realized.

The credit for seeing this potential and developing the themes and characters which later become standard in elegy is generally given to Gallus. He is mentioned as a predecessor by both Propertius[11] and Ovid,[12] who puts him first chronologically in his list of elegists. Unfortunately only ten lines of his poetry survive, nine of which came to light only recently in a papyrus find from Egypt. The reason for the loss of his works was his political disgrace in 27 BC when, as prefect of Egypt, he was recalled to Rome by Augustus for rashly claiming for himself the credit for some of Augustus' own achievements. He took his own life and following his disgrace his works were burned, although some copies must have survived as his elegies were known to Quintilian in the next century. Gallus belonged to the generation after Catullus and was a friend and contemporary of Virgil. In Virgil's tenth *Eclogue*, dedicated to Gallus, we have some hints about what his elegies would have been like. Servius, the fifth-century commentator on Virgil, tells us that Gallus wrote four books of elegies dedicated to the mime actress Lycoris, whose real name was Cytheris. In his *Eclogue* 10.42–8 Virgil has Gallus complaining to the shepherds of Arcadia of Lycoris' cruelty.[13] At *Eclogue* 6.64–73 Gallus is spoken of as about to attempt an aetiological poem on a mythological subject, the Grynean Grove. Whether this mythological poetry formed part of his elegies to Lycoris or whether it was composed separately we do not know, but Quintilian's description of his elegies as 'rather harsh' could refer to their learned mythological content. We know the mid-first-century BC Greek author and critic Parthenius dedicated to Gallus his prose collection of mythological love stories *Erotika Pathemata*, for use in 'epic or elegy'. Gallus, then, probably continued the tradition begun by Catullus of using mythology to illustrate one's own emotional experience. This becomes a standard feature of later elegy, especially in the work of Propertius.

[11] Propertius 2.34.91–2.
[12] Ovid, *Tristia* 4.10.53.
[13] Servius comments that 'all these verses are taken from Gallus' own poems'. Even if this is not taken literally, it is clear that the verses give us some indication of the main themes of Gallus' elegy, many of which occur in the later elegists. So the wish to grow old with one's mistress in the countryside is reminiscent of Tibullus (1.6.85–6); the opposition of love and war is common to all the elegists; the theme of the mistress's absence in a cold and distant land becomes the subject of Propertius 1.8.

Of the three surviving elegists, Propertius and Tibullus were rough contemporaries and Ovid was some ten years younger. Propertius came from a similar background socially to Tibullus. He belonged to a well-to-do provincial family from Assisi. His father died early and his family property suffered in Octavian's confiscations of 41–40 BC. He wrote four books of elegies, the first published in 28 BC; the second, as we now have it, may originally have consisted of two books, the first (poems 1–12) published in 26 BC and the second (poems 13–end) in 24 BC; the third book was published in 23 or 22 BC and the fourth somewhat later, around 16 BC, after Tibullus' death. Propertius is best known as a love poet, celebrating his devotion to a mistress called Cynthia, probably a pseudonym for a certain Hostia. The love theme becomes progressively less important as he widens the themes treated, so that by the fourth book there are only two Cynthia poems (7 and 8) among a collection of aetiological poems based on Rome and its history and influenced by the Alexandrian Greek poet Callimachus and such contemporary poems as Tibullus 2.5. He shares with Tibullus the images of love as a form of slavery, as a sickness, or as a form of military service. He makes greater use than Tibullus of mythological themes to illustrate his own affairs. A number of echoes and similarities between Propertius and Tibullus are discussed in the notes. Even given their relative chronology it is not always possible to tell who is echoing whom. We always have to bear in mind that poets could have heard private recitals of individual poems before they were put together in a book.

In the case of Ovid's *Amores* it is clear that the main influence must have been that of Tibullus on Ovid. The latest datable event mentioned in the three-book edition of Ovid's *Amores* (*Love Poems*), not published until 2 BC, is the death of Tibullus in 19 or 18 BC, in *Amores* 3.9, an elegy devoted entirely to Tibullus and his work on the occasion of his death. However, we know from an epigram attached to our edition of the *Amores* that this work had originally appeared as a five-book collection, which has not come down to us. Work on this five-book edition could have begun as early as 26–25 BC, after Tibullus's first book, but before his second, which it could have influenced. Ovid was born in March 43 BC into a family of equestrian status, like that of Tibullus. Around 26 BC, at the age of 17, he began to receive encouragement from Tibullus' aristocratic patron,

Messalla, and would certainly have known Tibullus and his con-
temporaries and heard them reciting their works in Messalla's
literary circle. The civil wars had been brought to an end in 31 BC,
when Ovid was only 12, and so, unlike Tibullus and Propertius, his
works show little trace of the horrors of war. He was born into an era
of new optimism and of great literary activity. Poets were active not
only in the circle of Messalla, but also in the circle of Maecenas,
where, as Ovid came of age, Horace had completed his *Epodes* and
Satires and Virgil his *Eclogues* and *Georgics*. Horace's *Odes* and
Virgil's *Aeneid* were in progress and Propertius, still outside the
circle of Maecenas at this stage, was working on his early poems.

Coming at the end of the tradition of Latin elegy, Ovid, in his
Amores addressed to his mistress Corinna, could no longer afford to
take the conventions of the genre seriously. His light-hearted and
sophisticated elegies often depend on giving a new or unexpected
turn to traditional themes. Love had become to some extent a
literary game, and symptomatic of this attitude is the fact that Ovid
begins and ends his *Amores* by surrendering to and taking leave
from, not his mistress, but love elegy itself. Like Tibullus, whom we
see from *Amores* 3.9 he greatly admired, he was often able to take a
detached, humorous view of the lover's persona, often undermining
at the end of a poem a position he had been carefully building up in
the course of it (e.g. *Amores* 1.10) or placing side by side poems of
conflicting purpose (e.g. *Amores* 2.7 and 2.8). By refusing to take love
elegy seriously Ovid effectively brought an end to the genre. Except
for the poems of Book 3 of the Tibullan corpus (see below) no
subsequent attempt was made to revive it, and Ovid himself applied
the elegiac metre to other genres of poetry.

Tibullus' Addressees

Whereas Cynthia is the mistress addressed in all four of Propertius'
books of elegies and Corinna is the mistress addressed by Ovid in all
three books of his *Amores*, Tibullus is unique among the elegists in
addressing a different mistress in each book (Delia in 1 and Nemesis
in 2) and in including in his collection homosexual poems addressed
to the boy Marathus (1.4, 1.8, 1.9). The dividing line between art
and life is particularly difficult to define in Roman elegy, which

combines real life with literary convention, so it is impossible to discuss the 'real' identity and status of the mistresses. Apuleius, writing in the first century AD, gives the identities of Catullus' Lesbia as Clodia, Propertius' Cynthia as Hostia, and Tibullus' Delia as Plania, and this convention of inventing a metrically equivalent pseudonym for the mistress seems to have been well developed. We have already seen that Gallus used the name Lycoris for his mistress Volumnia's stage name Cytheris. Apuleius, writing so much later than the elegists, is an unreliable witness, and although the identification of Catullus' Lesbia with Clodia Metelli is now generally accepted, the identification of Cynthia with Hostia and Delia with Plania is far from secure. Plania, in fact, is nothing more than a translation into Latin of the Greek Delia (Greek *delos* = Latin *planus*, meaning 'clear', 'bright'). The fact that Apuleius makes no attempt to identify Nemesis, Marathus, or Ovid's Corinna suggests that these may have been literary composites with no basis in any one real-life partner.

The name Delia, like the name Cynthia in Propertius, was perhaps intended to suggest a connection between the mistress and poetic inspiration by bringing to mind the god Apollo, in his guise as the god of poetry and music; his home was on the island of Delos (from which Delia), where he had a shrine on Mount Cynthus (from which Cynthia). Another possible association for Delia would be with the goddess Diana, sister of Apollo and also from Delos. Virgil first uses the epithet Delia for Diana in *Eclogue* 7.29, and the name is applied to the mistress of the shepherd Menalcas in *Eclogue* 3.67. Given the strong influence of Virgil's *Eclogues* on Tibullus' first book, where Delia is associated with an idyllic life in a pastoral setting (see especially 1.5.21–34), Tibullus could well have taken the name and its associations from Virgil. Like Delia, Diana was associated with the unspoilt countryside and through her association with the moon, Luna, with brightness and light. We will see later how the 'bright' Delia is the perfect foil for the 'dark' Nemesis of Book 2, associated by Hesiod with the daughter of Night. The marital status of Delia is discussed at 1.6.67–8 where it is made clear that she does not have the braided hair and the long robe of a married Roman *matrona*. In 1.2.43 and 1.6.15 and 33 she is shown as living with a man described as her *coniunx*, which can mean either

'husband' or simply 'current lover'. Since she was not a married
woman she must simply have been the man's concubine. As it would
be very unusual for a freeborn female citizen to live in such a
relationship, her status is likely to have been that of a *libertina* or
freedwoman. This status would fit in well with her worship of Isis
(1.3.23–4), a cult favoured by freedwomen rather than free female
citizens.

The name Nemesis as a personification for retribution occurs
frequently in Hellenistic epigram. As a goddess of the Hellenistic
period Nemesis is often represented holding in her hand a wheel.
This so-called Wheel of Fortune represents the fickleness of fate.
The rich become poor and vice versa; more relevant for elegy, the
successful lover is replaced by a rival. A key theme of Tibullus' first
book is the way no one lover is successful for long, but each in turn is
replaced by a rival. It is Tibullus' *nemesis* in Book 2 to become
enslaved to a cruel urban mistress who causes him to abandon many
of the cherished ideals that had characterized his affair with Delia.
From a literary point of view this change of mistress in Book 2 has
a number of advantages, allowing Tibullus to explore love from a
different perspective in each. The pious and naïve idealist of the first
book becomes the cynical and more predatory person of the second.
The social status of Nemesis, who in 2.3.59–60 has taken up with an
ex-slave, is conceived to be the same as that of Delia, namely a
freedwoman. Although neither Delia nor Nemesis can be associated
as closely with a 'real' person as Catullus' Lesbia, the possibility
that certain episodes such as Delia's sickness in 1.5 or the death of
Nemesis' sister in 2.6 were taken from real-life events cannot be
dismissed entirely.

In including three poems concerning his love for the boy
Marathus, Tibullus is closer to Greek epigram than to his fellow
Roman elegists. Both Callimachus and Meleager addressed some of
their epigrams to boys. In Latin there are precedents in Catullus'
poems to the boy Juventius and in Virgil's second *Eclogue* on
the subject of the rustic Corydon's love for the city boy Alexis.
Propertius recommends affairs with boys for his friends (2.4), but
not for himself and his only mention of the theme comes in his
mythological narrative of the story of Hylas in 1.20. Similarly Ovid
in *Ars* 2.683–4 says that boys could be a suitable topic for elegy, but

he rejects the theme for himself and no such poems occur in his *Amores*. The topic would possibly have seemed out of place in collections devoted to a single mistress. Tibullus is more interested in exploring love from a number of different angles, as we have seen in his choice of addressing a new mistress in Book 2, and the Marathus poems serve to expand his range of effects, especially in Elegies 1.8 and 1.9 where matters are complicated further by the love of Marathus for the girl Pholoe. The name Marathus is Greek in origin and suitable for a slave boy. It occurs in real life as the name of a freedman of Augustus, a certain Iulius Marathus. Scholars have discussed its possible meanings and significance, especially in connection with its first occurrence at 1.4.81: *Alas, Marathus slowly tortures me with love*. It may have been connected with the Greek *marathos* = 'fennel', either because this plant was supposed to possess aphrodisiac qualities or because, when dried, it was used for kindling or for carrying flames. Others think that the physical appearance of the plant with its long, thin stem could have suggested a youth pining away for love. Some scholars reject the connection with the plant and see in Marathus a derivation from the Greek verb *marainomai*, 'to die down'. In their view Marathus would torture Tibullus by allowing the fire of his passion to die down. Multiple explanations have been offered and no single one is entirely satisfactory; Tibullus himself may have had a number of different associations in mind when choosing the name.

Other characters named or addressed in the elegies are discussed in the notes to the poems in which they appear.[14]

Tibullus' Books as Poetic Units: Structure, Character, and Themes

BOOK I

Like Horace with the ten poems of his first book of *Satires* and Virgil with his ten *Eclogues*, Tibullus would have arranged the ten poems of his first book of elegies in a meaningful order, which would not necessarily reflect their chronological order of composition. Often

[14] These are, in order of appearance: Messalla, Tibullus' patron; Titius, friend of Tibullus; Pholoe, girlfriend of Marathus; Cornutus, friend of Tibullus; Messalinus, Messalla's son; Macer, a poet and contemporary of Tibullus; Phryne, Nemesis' madam.

correspondences can be seen between the end of one poem and the beginning of the next in the collection.[15] Individual poems would then take on added significance by being read as part of a narrative sequence. Thus the first book as a whole can be seen as tracing a development from the pacifist ideal of love in the country with a faithful mistress, as presented in 1.1, to the mature realization by the end of the book that such an ideal could never be fulfilled. The book is carefully constructed. Elegies 1 and 10 are closely linked and contrasted. Then two pairs of Delia poems 2 + 3 and 5 + 6 are separated by 4, which introduces the Marathus theme. Between the end poem of the Delia cycle 6 and the two main poems of the Marathus cycle 8 and 9 comes Elegy 7, the hinge on which the whole book turns, dedicated to Tibullus' patron Messalla on the occasion of his birthday and triumph over Aquitania. In the first two Delia poems, 2 and 3, it is external threats that keep her and Tibullus apart. In 2 her current lover, the *coniunx*, has locked Delia away in his town house and in 3 Tibullus is sick abroad while absent on military duties with Messalla. The light-hearted Elegy 4 on pederasty comes as a complete surprise and interrupts the development of the Delia theme. Elegies 5 and 6 mark the end of the Delia affair and reveal a progressive deterioration in the relationship. In 5 Tibullus realizes his dreams of an ideal existence in the country with Delia to have been in vain as a rich rival, probably identical with the *coniunx* in 2, has replaced him in Delia's affections. At this stage Delia herself is not blamed, but rather the wicked bawd who has led her astray. In the final poem of the cycle, Elegy 6, it is Delia herself who has taken a new lover (lines 5–6) and deceives both Tibullus and her *coniunx* with the tricks that Tibullus himself had taught her earlier in the affair. This initiates Tibullus' central theme of the Wheel of Fortune,[16] which, as we have seen, represents the instability of relationships and the constant replacement of one lover

---

[15] See introductory note to 1.5 on the connection between the opening of this poem and the end of 1.4; note to 1.6.6 on the connection between 1.5 and 1.6 and introductory note to 1.9 for links between 1.8 and 1.9.

[16] Named in 1.5.70. For a detailed discussion of this topic in Tibullus see R. Maltby, 'The Wheel of Fortune: Nemesis and the Central Poems of Tibullus I and II', in S. Kyriakidis and Francesco de Martino (eds.), *Middles in Latin Poetry* (Bari: Levante, 2005), 103–21.

by another. This Wheel was connected in mythology with Nemesis, the goddess of retribution, and the name of Tibullus' mistress in the second book. After the end of the Delia cycle comes Elegy 7 addressed to Messalla. This poem contains no mention of Tibullus' love affairs, but shows his patron's military and diplomatic exploits in a positive light, emphasizing their benefit to the community as a whole, and culminating in his contribution to the rebuilding of a public highway, the Via Latina. The initial rejection of war with which the book begins, Elegy 1, has been shown in Elegy 3 to be impossible. Nor is the rejection of war and the wealth it brings compatible with success in love, as Delia's choice of a rich soldier in 2 and 5 and the boy's demands for rich gifts in 4 have shown. In the Marathus cycle which follows Elegy 7 the same principles of nemesis which operated in the case of the Delia affair are shown to apply. In 8 Tibullus claims to support Marathus in his affair with the girl Pholoe, but just as Marathus had made fools of his lovers, including Tibullus, in the past so Pholoe now makes a fool of him. Pholoe also is warned not to be too harsh on the boy, as such behaviour could result in suffering for her by way of retribution. This theme of retribution links Elegies 8 and 9, with the suffering that awaits Pholoe at the end of 8 being picked up at the beginning of 9 by a threat of retribution on the addressee of that poem. The Wheel of Fortune has now turned full circle. A boy has betrayed Tibullus with a rich old lover whose young wife betrays him with a boy. None of the characters are named, but given the close connection between Elegies 8 and 9 the most economical solution would be to see the boy as Marathus and the rich old man's young wife as Pholoe, who deceives him with Marathus. The end of these two love cycles is marked at 1.9.82–3 by Tibullus' dedicating an offering to Venus as one who is 'freed from love' (*resolutus amore*). Elegy 10 with its rejection of war and prayer to a personified Peace echoes many of the themes of Elegy 1, but there are two significant differences. First, whereas in Elegy 1 Tibullus rejects war out of hand, in Elegy 10 he is dragged off to war against his will. Secondly, the theme of elegiac love for the mistress Delia, a prominent part of the ideal of 1.1, is rejected in favour of the old Roman ideal of family life with children (39–44), a theme touched upon in the Messalla poem at 1.7.55ff), and to appear again in the marriage poem for Cornutus in 2.2. The

ideas presented in this first book are in many ways consistent with
the new Augustan ideal: retirement from society into a Golden Age
of idleness and elegiac love has to be rejected in favour of civic
duty and the restoration of peace and moral integrity to society as
a whole.

BOOK 2

We do not know whether Tibullus had completed his second book at
the time of his death. It has only six poems and 430 lines, as com-
pared with ten poems and 808 lines for Book 1. There are, however,
precedents for collections of six in Callimachus' six *Hymns*, the six
books of Lucretius' *De Rerum Natura* and at a later date in the six
poems of Lygdamus, that begin Book 3 of the *Corpus Tibullianum*,
and the six poems of Statius' first book of *Silvae*. Whether or not it
was complete on Tibullus' death the book shows signs of careful
construction. First there are deliberate echoes which link it to the
first book, with 2.6 being carefully linked with 2.1 (see introductory
note to 2.6) and 1.10 to 2.1 (see note to 1.10.29). Within the book
beginnings and endings of consecutive poems are linked.[17] The six
poems contained in the book fall into two balanced groups: three
on rites or ceremonies at which the poet presides (1, 2, and 5) are
balanced by three dramatic monologues concerning his affair with
Nemesis (3, 4, and 6). There is an alternation between long and
short poems, with 2 being Tibullus' shortest and 5 his longest elegy.
The ceremonial poems 1, 2, and 5 preserve the values which have
become familiar from Book 1: country life and traditional religion,
the importance of poetry and the arts and of family life and married
love. In the Nemesis poems, by contrast, these themes and attitudes
are often reversed. In 2.3 the countryside is no longer an idyllic
setting for love, but a harsh place of servile labour that separates
Tibullus from his mistress; the main gods of the countryside, Ceres
and Bacchus, venerated in 2.1, are cursed (2.3.61–6); a diatribe
against wealth and war (2.3.35–47) is undermined by a willingness
to espouse wealth to provide Nemesis with the luxuries needed
for urban living (2.3.49–62). The Muses, previously looked up to

---

[17] See introductory note to 2.2 on links with the end of 2.1; note to 2.3.1 on links with
the end of 2.2; introductory note to 2.4 on links with the end of 2.3.

(1.4.65–8), are dismissed at 2.4.15 in the same words that military life was dismissed in 1.1.75–6. Venus herself, the object of a personal cult of Tibullus in the first book, is to have her temple sacked to provide Nemesis with gifts (2.4.21–6). Even his ancestral home and family gods, the *Lares*, so important a feature of his ideal in the first book, are to be sold at Nemesis' bidding (2.4.53–4). The farewell to warfare in favour of Venus with which the first poem of Book 1 ends (1.1.71–4) is replaced by an attempt in the last poem of Book 2 to bid farewell to Venus in favour of war (2.6.9–10); but Love forces him against his will to return to Nemesis. The gloom with which the final poem of the Nemesis cycle ends (2.6.49–54) contrasts with the faint glimmer of hope for love in old age with which the Delia cycle had ended (1.6.85–6). The choice of a new mistress in the second book enabled Tibullus to explore love from a more cynical angle, closer in some respects to attitudes to be found in Propertius and Ovid.

BOOK 3 OF THE TIBULLAN CORPUS

The text of Tibullus has come down to us in three books, only the first two of which are by Tibullus himself. As we have seen, Tibullus' second book was published shortly after his death in late 18 or early 19 BC. By contrast, most of the poems in Book 3 show the influence of Ovid and were probably published after Ovid's death in AD 17. The reason they were transmitted with Tibullus' work is unclear, but some of the writers included may have been connected with Messalla and his family, and certainly a number of their poems show the influence of Tibullus. As no poem in this book can be shown to have been written by Tibullus, it is not included in the present translation.

The book begins with six poems by a writer who gives his name as Lygdamus, addressed to a woman named Neaera and describing the breakdown of an affair with this lady, who is depicted as a wife or, at least, a social equal. They appear to have been composed by a post-Ovidian elegist who wished to take the conventions of elegy into the new area of married love.

The next poem in Book 3, poem 3.7, is an anonymous panegyric for Messalla on the occasion of his promotion to the consulship in 31 BC. Its position in the book would make it parallel to Tibullus' birthday poem for Messalla (1.7), just as the six Lygdamus poems could be seen as parallel to the six Delia poems at the beginning of Tibullus' first book. On metrical and stylistic grounds this panegyric could not have been composed in the time of Tibullus (its dramatic date) or even by Lygdamus, but was probably a school exercise produced in the Flavian period, possibly at the suggestion of one of Messalla's descendants.

The following five poems (3.8–12) are referred to as the Sulpicia cycle. Composed by an anonymous poet, they take as their subject the love of Sulpicia for a certain Cerinthus. In poems 8, 10, and 12 the poet speaks in his own voice, while poems 9 and 11 are spoken in the voice of Sulpicia. These appear to have been composed before those of Lygdamus, shortly after the death of Ovid in the early first century AD.

Poems 13–18 of the third book are shorter than the poems of the Sulpicia cycle, the longest being only 10 lines, and on stylistic grounds seem to have been written by a different poet. In 3.16.4 this poet identifies herself as Sulpicia, daughter of Servius, and in 3.14.5 she refers to Messalla as a close relative (*propinque*). The most likely person fitting this description would be Messalla's niece, daughter of his sister Valeria, who was married to Servius Sulpicius Rufus. The six short poems concern her love for a certain Cerinthus, possibly to be identified with the Cornutus of Tibullus 2.2 (both names being derived from words meaning 'horn'). The language resembles the polite conversational language of the aristocratic elite and the metre follows Ovidian practice. It could well be that these are the oldest poems in the third book, perhaps inspiring the later Sulpicia cycle, written by Messalla's niece in the last decade of the first century BC.

The poet of 3.19 names himself as Tibullus (line 13), but there are echoes of Ovid's late work and metrical practice which mean it cannot have been written by Tibullus. A final poem (3.20) on the theme of the poet's wish to hear tales of his mistress's unfaithfulness again is Ovidian in style and metre and possibly dates from the early first century AD.

The third book, then, consists of different groups of poems, written at different times, but skilfully woven together into a complete unit. Many are Tibullan in inspiration, although Ovid is also a major influence. It is possible the collection was connected in some way to the family archive of Tibullus' patron Messalla and his descendants.

Tibullus' Later Influence[18]

At the time of his death Tibullus' literary reputation was high, as is indicated by the epigram of Domitius Marsus quoted above and by the famous elegy (*Amores* 3.9) composed by Ovid to mark his death. In the next generation Velleius Paterculus (2.36.3), writing under Tiberius, brackets Tibullus with Ovid as both being 'most perfect in the form of their work' (*perfectissimi in forma operis sui*). In the last decade of the first century AD Quintilian (*Inst.* 10.1.93) describes Tibullus as *tersus atque elegans*, 'elegant and to the point', and ranks him first among the Roman elegists. The poets Martial and Statius, contemporaries of Quintilian, admired Tibullus and alluded to his works, and the not infrequent echoes of his verse on metrical epitaphs of the time attest to his popularity with the general reading public. In the second century there are no notable literary echoes of Tibullus, though the inclusion of his life at this period in Suetonius' 'Lives of Distinguished Men' may have led to a renewal of interest. Certainly Apuleius at this time was still able to inform us (*Apol.* 10) that Delia's real name was Plania. In the third and fourth centuries references to Tibullus are rare, although occasional echoes in Nemesianus and Ausonius show us that he was still being read. The last author to mention him in the ancient world was Sidonius Apollinaris in the fifth century (*Carm.* 9.260, *Epist.* 2.10.6), though his brief mentions do not prove direct knowledge of his poems.

In the Renaissance direct literary echoes in the Latin poetry of the period begin at the end of the fourteenth and continue into the sixteenth century. Numerous editions of his work were published before 1700, but although his poems must have been known in cultivated literary circles they left little impression on the vernacular literature of the time. In England there are odd echoes in the works of Spenser, and Tibullus is mentioned by Herrick and Burton. In France at the same period the picture is pretty much the same with

---

[18] Readers interested in Tibullan reception should read the more detailed discussion in K. Smith, *The Elegies of Albius Tibullus* (New York: The American Book Company, 1913), 58–64.

mentions in Rabelais and Montaigne and occasional echoes in the
poets of the Pléiade, such as Ronsard and Belleau. In Italy Tibullan
influence was stronger, with frequent echoes of his work in such
writers as Sannazaro, Ariosto, and Tasso, and especially in the *Elegie*
of Luigi Alamanni, published in 1532. The popularity of Tibullus in
Europe increased in the eighteenth century, which combined formal
classicism with a particular penchant for pastoral love poetry. This
interest in Tibullan elegy continued in Germany into the nineteenth
century, when a number of translations into German were published
along with no less than four annotated editions of his work. In
modern times Tibullus' popularity has been eclipsed to some extent
by that of Propertius and Ovid. This is a situation which the present
translation hopes to rectify.

NOTE ON THE TEXT

EVIDENCE for the text of Tibullus is late in comparison with the
texts of other classical authors such as Terence or Virgil.[1] It is based
mainly on a number of complete manuscripts, the earliest of which
goes back only to the end of the fourteenth century. In addition there
are a number of excerpts in medieval florilegia, the most important
of which were put together in the eleventh and twelfth centuries.
All our complete manuscripts transmit the third book of the corpus
along with the genuine Tibullan books 1 and 2. One fragmentary
manuscript (known as F), now lost, contained only the second half
of the third book. Current studies of the text of Tibullus suggest
that all our manuscripts of the complete text can be traced back to
one single codex, brought from France to Italy, possibly by Petrarch,
at some time in the fourteenth century. A copy of this codex,
probably written in 1374, was obtained by Coluccio Salutati. This
copy still exists in the Ambrosian library in Milan (Mediolanensis
Ambrosianus R sup., conventionally referred to as A) and provides
us with our oldest datable evidence for the full text.

In editing the text the most important witness is therefore A,
although the older florilegia may sometimes retain true readings not
to be found in A. There is no evidence that any full manuscript later
than A is independent of it, so readings in these manuscripts which
differ from A must have the status of conjectures. In the present
edition, which is based on a new investigation of the manuscript
evidence, readings from later manuscripts were used only when
correcting obvious errors in A. For further details, see the Textual
Notes, pp. 124–9.

---

[1] For a detailed discussion of the textual transmission of Tibullus see Rouse and
Reeve (1983), 420–5.

TRANSLATOR'S NOTE

My aim in this translation is to replicate the form, depth, and grace of Tibullus' verse while preserving as much of the meaning and metaphor as possible. Rather than translate in free verse I have tried to replicate the elegiac couplet with alternating lines of iambic hexameter and iambic pentameter for which I have allowed myself ample traditional substitutions, such as a trochee for an iamb in the first foot and liberal spondaic substitutions. As is customary in English formal poetry, I have also used trochaic substitutions to signal mood changes. When I have ended a line on a feminine ending, I have generally, but not always, followed it with a headless line unless there was a pause at the end of the line. Since I tried to retain original names and places wherever possible, I have accepted that this choice occasionally affects the metre and I have minimized the metrical irregularities when I could not eliminate them. Where I have supplied lines that are missing in the Latin, these are set within square brackets.

The musicality of Tibullus' verse comes in part from skilled use of alliteration and assonance, which I have tried to imitate where possible. He also used internal rhyme and some strikingly unusual end-rhyme, which I have also tried to duplicate. I have also imitated puns and other wordplay when I could.

I want to acknowledge my admiration for and heavy reliance on the Murgatroyd, Putnam, and Maltby commentaries. It has been an honour and a pleasure to work with Robert Maltby himself on the final version of this book, and he suggested a number of significant improvements. Alicia Stallings, as always, made herself available for assistance on knotty lines. Laura Mali-Astrue provided considerable insight, particularly on some of the odder points. David Ferry, Deborah Warren, and Rachel Hadas read early drafts and provided useful comments. Aaron Poochigian did a painstakingly careful line-by-line review of the accuracy of the first complete draft and spared me from countless humiliating mistakes. Artemis Kirk assisted me with access to resources through Georgetown University's Lauinger Library. My workshop colleagues at Eratosphere and the Powow

River Poets also provided comments on several sections. Finally, I am grateful to Judith Luna of Oxford University Press for her enthusiastic support of this project. In other words, a good translation is impossible without a lot of help from a lot of smart friends.

SELECT BIBLIOGRAPHY

General Background Works

Barsby, J. A., *Ovid's Amores Book One* (Oxford: Clarendon Press, 1973).

Booth, J., *Latin Love Elegy: A Companion to Translations of A. G. Lee* (Bristol: Bristol Classical Press, 1995).

Brown, M., *Horace Satires I* (Warminster: Aris & Phillips, 1993).

Cairns, F., *Generic Composition in Greek and Roman Poetry* (Edinburgh: Edinburgh University Press, 1972).

Copley, F., *Exclusus Amator: A Study in Latin Love Poetry* (Baltimore: American Philological Association, 1956).

Dalby, A., *Empires of Pleasure: Luxury and Indulgence in the Roman World* (London: Routledge, 2000).

Day, A. A., *The Origins of Latin Love-Elegy* (Oxford: Blackwell, 1938).

Fear, T., 'The Poet as Pimp: Elegiac Seduction in the Time of Augustus', *Arethusa* 33 (2000), 217–40.

Galinsky, K., *Augustan Culture: An Interpretive Introduction* (Princeton: Princeton University Press, 1996).

Gold, B. K. (ed.), *Literary and Artistic Patronage in Ancient Rome* (Austin: University of Texas Press, 1982).

Griffin, J., *Latin Poets and Roman Life* (London: Duckworth, 1985).

Hinds, S., *Allusion and Intertext: Dynamics of Appropriation in Roman Poetry* (Cambridge: Cambridge University Press, 1998).

James, S., *Learned Girls and Male Persuasion* (Berkeley: University of California Press, 2003).

Kennedy, D., *The Arts of Love: Five Studies in the Discourse of Roman Love Elegy* (Cambridge: Cambridge University Press, 1993).

Lilja, S., *The Roman Elegists' Attitude to Women* (New York: Garland Publishing, 1978).

Liveley, G., and Salzman-Mitchell, P., *Latin Elegy and Narratology: Fragments of Story* (Columbus: Ohio State University Press, 2008).

Luck, G., *The Latin Love Elegy* (London: Methuen & Co., 1959).

Lyne, R. O. A. M., *The Latin Love Poets: From Catullus to Horace* (Oxford: Clarendon Press, 1980).

Maltby, R., *Latin Love Elegy* (Bristol: Bristol Classical Press, 1980).

Miller, P., *Subjecting Verses: Latin Love Elegy and the Emergence of the Real* (Princeton: Princeton University Press, 2004).

Muecke, F., *Horace Satires II* (Warminster: Aris & Phillips, 1993).

Newman, J. K., *Augustus and the New Poetry* (Brussels: Latomus, 1967).

Ramsby, T., *Textual Permanence: Roman Elegists and the Epigraphic Tradition* (London: Duckworth, 2007).

Ross, D., *Backgrounds to Augustan Poetry: Gallus, Elegy and Rome* (Cambridge: Cambridge University Press, 1975).

Sime, R., *The Augustan Aristocracy* (Oxford: Clarendon Press, 1986).

Sullivan, J. P. (ed.), *Critical Essays on Roman Literature: Elegy and Lyric* (London: Routledge, 1962).

Veyne, P., *Roman Erotic Poetry: Love, Poetry and the West*, trans. D. Pellauer (Chicago: University of Chicago Press, 1988).

Whitaker, R., *Myth and Personal Experience in Roman Love-Elegy* (Göttingen: Vandenhoeck and Ruprecht, 1983).

Williams, G., *Tradition and Originality in Roman Poetry* (Oxford: Clarendon Press, 1968).

Wyke, M., *The Roman Mistress: Ancient and Modern Representations* (Oxford: Oxford University Press, 2001).

Background Works Specifically on Tibullus

Ball, R. J., *Tibullus the Elegist: A Critical Survey*, Hypomnemata 77 (Göttingen, 1983).

Bright, D., *Haec Mihi Fingebam: Tibullus in his World*. (Leiden: E. J. Brill, 1978).

Cairns, F., *Tibullus: A Hellenistic Poet at Rome* (Cambridge: Cambridge University Press, 1979).

Lee-Stecum, P., *Powerplay in Tibullus* (Cambridge: Cambridge University Press, 1998).

Maltby, R., 'Tibullus and the Language of Latin Elegy', in J. N. Adams and R. G. Mayer (eds.), *Proceedings of the British Academy 93: Aspects of the Language of Latin Poetry* (Oxford: Clarendon Press, 1999), 377–98.

—— 'Technical Language in Tibullus', *Emerita* 67 (1999), 231–49.

—— 'Tibullus 2.5 and the Early History of Rome', *Kleos* 7 (2002), 291–304.

—— 'The Wheel of Fortune: Nemesis and the Central Poems of Tibullus I and II', in S. Kyriakidis and Francesco de Martino (eds.), *Middles in Latin Poetry* (Bari: Levante, 2005), 103–21.

—— and Booth, J., 'Light and Dark: Play on *candidus* and Related Concepts in the Elegies of Tibullus', *Mnemosyne* 58 (2005), 124–31.

Rouse, R. H., and Reeve, M. D., 'Tibullus', in L. D. Reynolds (ed.), *Texts and Transmissions: A Survey of the Latin Classics* (Oxford: Clarendon Press, 1983), 420–5.

Solmsen, F., 'Tibullus as an Augustan Poet', *Hermes* 90 (1962), 295–325.

Annotated Editions of Tibullus

Maltby, R., *Tibullus: Elegies* (Cambridge: Francis Cairns Ltd., 2002).

Murgatroyd, P., *Tibullus I: A Commentary on the First Book of the Elegies of Albius Tibullus* (Pietermaritzburg: University of Natal Press, 1980).

—— *Tibullus, Elegies II* (Oxford: Clarendon Press, 1994).

Putnam, M., *Tibullus: A Commentary* (Norman: University of Oklahoma Press, 1973).

Smith, K., *The Elegies of Albius Tibullus* (New York: The American Book Company, 1913).

Translations of Tibullus

Carrier, C., *The Poems of Tibullus* (Bloomington: Indiana University Press, 1968).

Dunlop, P., *The Poems of Tibullus with the Tibullan Collection* (London: Penguin Books, 1972).

Goold, G., *Catullus, Tibullus, Pervigilium Veneris* (Cambridge, Mass.: Harvard University Press, 1913. J. P. Postgate translated the section on Tibullus).

Lee, G., *Tibullus: Elegies* (Leeds: Francis Cairns, 1995).

Shea, G., *Delia and Nemesis: The Elegies of Albius Tibullus* (Lanham, Md.: University Press of America, 1998).

Further Reading in Oxford World's Classics

Horace, *The Complete Odes and Epodes*, trans. David West.

Ovid, *The Love Poems (Amores)*, trans. A. D. Melville, ed. E. J. Kenney.

Propertius, *The Poems*, trans. Guy Lee, introduction by R. O. A. M. Lyne.

Virgil, *The Eclogues and Georgics*, trans. C. Day-Lewis, introduction by R. O. A. M. Lyne.

—— *Georgics*, trans. Peter Fallon, introduction by Elaine Fantham.

A CHRONOLOGY OF TIBULLUS

All dates are BC.

55–49   Birth of Tibullus.

55   Death of Lucretius.

54   Death of Catullus.

49   Caesar crosses the Rubicon to become Roman dictator.

44   Murder of Caesar by Brutus and Cassius.

43   Birth of Ovid. Murder of Cicero.

42   Brutus and Cassius defeated by Antony and Octavian at Philippi.

41–40   Tibullus' family estate suffers in Octavian's land confiscations.

38   Publication of Virgil's *Eclogues*, which mention Gallus' love poetry.

31   Octavian defeats Antony at Actium. Consulship of Octavian and Messalla.

30   Gallus appointed Prefect of Egypt by Octavian.

29   Publication of Virgil's *Georgics*.

28   Publication of Propertius Book 1.

27   Messalla's triumph over Aquitania. Octavian takes the title Augustus.

27–26   Publication of Tibullus Book 1.

26   Gallus recalled from Egypt in disgrace and commits suicide in Rome.

26–24   Publication of Propertius Book 2, probably originally in two books.

23   Publication of Horace, *Odes* Books 1–3. First edition of Ovid's *Amores* in five books.

22   Publication of Propertius Book 3.

19   Death of Virgil.

19–18   Death of Tibullus and publication of his Book 2.

ELEGIES

Book I

LIBER PRIMUS

1

Diuitias alius fuluo sibi congerat auro
  et teneat culti iugera magna soli,
quem labor assiduus uicino terreat hoste,
  Martia cui somnos classica pulsa fugent:
me mea paupertas uitae traducat inerti
  dum meus assiduo luceat igne focus.
ipse seram teneras maturo tempore uites
  rusticus et facili grandia poma manu,
nec Spes destituat, sed frugum semper aceruos
  praebeat et pleno pinguia musta lacu: 10
nam ueneror seu stipes habet desertus in agris
  seu uetus in triuio florida serta lapis,
et quodcumque mihi pomum nouus educat annus
  libatum agricolam ponitur ante deum.
flaua Ceres, tibi sit nostro de rure corona
  spicea quae templi pendeat ante fores
pomosisque ruber custos ponatur in hortis
  terreat ut saeua falce Priapus aues.
uos quoque, felicis quondam, nunc pauperis agri
  custodes, fertis munera uestra, Lares;   20
tunc uitula innumeros lustrabat caesa iuuencos,
  nunc agna exigui est hostia parua soli:
agna cadet uobis, quam circum rustica pubes
  clamet 'io, messes et bona uina date'.
iam modo, iam possim contentus uiuere paruo
  nec semper longae deditus esse uiae,
sed Canis aestiuos ortus uitare sub umbra
  arboris ad riuos praetereuntis aquae.
nec tamen interdum pudeat tenuisse bidentem
  aut stimulo tardos increpuisse boues;   30
non agnamue sinu pigeat fetumue capellae
  desertum oblita matre referre domum.

BOOK ONE

1

May someone else assemble wealth of gleaming gold
    and hold vast plots of cultivated land,
one who would fear the constant toil of lurking foes,
    one whose sleep flees when Mars' trumpets* blare.
May poverty provide me with an idle life
    while steady fire burns within my hearth.
In season may I plant tall fruit-trees and young vines
    myself—and with a farmhand's skilful touch.
May Hope not disappoint, but always send stacked crops
    and fill my vats with juice from bursting grapes   10
because I pray by lonely tree-stumps in the fields
    or weathered stone* at crossroads decked with flowers,
and all first fruit that is produced for me is offered
    as a gift before the farmer-god.*
Upon the temple threshold, golden Ceres,* may
    my farm-grown cornhusk crown be hung for you
and red Priapus* be on guard in fruitful gardens
    so his vicious scythe may scare off birds.
You, Lares,* also take in gifts as guardians
    of threadbare land that once was prosperous.*   20
Back then a slaughtered calf would bless vast herds; today's
    small victim is a lamb from meagre soil.
The lamb will die for you; around her country boys
    will cry, 'O give us crops and vintage wine!'
If only I could live with little, happy now
    at last, and not be given to long trips,
but shun the rising Dog Star's heat* in shade beneath
    a tree beside the ripples of a brook
and never feel ashamed to wield a hoe at times
    or scold reluctant cattle with a prod   30
or carry home a cradled baby goat or lamb
    abandoned by an inattentive mother.

at uos exiguo pecori, furesque lupique,
    parcite: de magno est praeda petenda grege.
hic ego pastoremque meum lustrare quotannis
    et placidam soleo spargere lacte Palem.
adsitis, diui, neu uos e paupere mensa
    dona nec e puris spernite fictilibus:
fictilia antiquus primum sibi fecit agrestis,
    pocula de facili conposuitque luto.   40
non ego diuitias patrum fructusque requiro
    quos tulit antiquo condita messis auo:
parua seges satis est, satis est requiescere lecto
    si licet et solito membra leuare toro.
quam iuuat immites uentos audire cubantem
    et dominam tenero continuisse sinu
aut gelidas hibernus aquas cum fuderit Auster
    securum somnos igne iuuante sequi.
hoc mihi contingat: sit diues iure furorem
    qui maris et tristes ferre potest pluuias.   50
o quantum est auri pereat potiusque smaragdi
    quam fleat ob nostras ulla puella uias!
te bellare decet terra, Messalla, marique
    ut domus hostiles praeferat exuuias:
me retinent uinctum formosae uincla puellae,
    et sedeo duras ianitor ante fores.
non ego laudari curo, mea Delia; tecum
    dum modo sim, quaeso segnis inersque uocer.
te spectem suprema mihi cum uenerit hora;
    te teneam moriens deficiente manu.   60
flebis et arsuro positum me, Delia, lecto,
    tristibus et lacrimis oscula mixta dabis.
flebis: non tua sunt duro praecordia ferro
    uincta nec in tenero stat tibi corde silex.
illo non iuuenis poterit de funere quisquam
    lumina non uirgo sicca referre domum.
tu manes ne laede meos sed parce solutis
    crinibus et teneris, Delia, parce genis.
interea, dum Fata sinunt, iungamus amores:
    iam ueniet tenebris Mors adoperta caput,   70

But all you wolves and robbers, spare my meagre flock!
   Pursue your plunder from some massive herd!
I purify my shepherd in this place each year
   and sprinkle gentle Pales with some milk.*
Gods, be with me, and never scorn what's offered from
   a humble table or clean earthenware—
an old-time countryman first fashioned for himself
   some earthen cups he made from pliant clay.   40
I do not miss my fathers' wealth or profits built
   from yields that my old grandfather had saved.
A small crop is enough; it is enough to rest
   in bed and loll upon familiar sheets.
How sweet it is while lying down to hear fierce winds
   and hold a mistress with a tender grasp!
Or when cold Austral winds* are spreading sleet, what joy
   to slumber safely with a fire's help!
Let this befall me: may wealth be earned by one
   who bears grim rain and seas that froth and foam.   50
O how much better that our gold and gems be lost
   than any girl be crying as we roam!
Messalla,* it is right *you* fight on land and sea
   so spoils of war* may decorate your home!
Chains of a gorgeous girl* restrain *me*, and I linger
   like a doorman* at her stubborn door.
I want no praise, my Delia;* if I am with you,
   I'm asking to be labelled weak and dull.
May I behold you* when my final hour comes;
   as I die, let me hold you as hands fail.   60
Delia, when flames engulf my bier you'll weep for me,
   and then you'll mix your kisses with sad tears.
You'll weep, for stubborn iron doesn't wrap your breast,
   nor is there flint inside your tender heart.
Nobody, neither man nor maiden, could return
   home from that funeral and be dry-eyed.
Do not do damage to my spirit! Delia, spare
   your unbound hair and spare your tender cheeks.*
Meanwhile, as long as fate allows, let's join in love!
   First Death will come, his features cloaked in gloom,*   70

iam subrepet iners aetas neque amare decebit
　　dicere nec cano blanditias capite.
nunc leuis est tractanda Venus dum frangere postes
　　non pudet et rixas inseruisse iuuat.
hic ego dux milesque bonus. uos, signa tubaeque,
　　ite procul; cupidis uulnera ferte uiris,
ferte et opes: ego composito securus aceruo
　　dites despiciam despiciamque famem.

then age will sneak up, and it won't be right to love
　or speak seductive words with snowy hair.
Lighthearted love must be indulged while there's no shame
　in breaking doors and brawling gives us pleasure.
I'm a good soldier and good leader* here. You troops
　and trumpets, move it! Bring harm to the greedy,
and bring their lucre! Made secure by stacks I stored,*
　I'll hate starvation and I'll hate great wealth.

2

Adde merum uinoque nouos compesce dolores,
　　occupet ut fessi lumina uicta sopor;
neu quisquam multo percussum tempora Baccho
　　excitet, infelix dum requiescit amor:
nam posita est nostrae custodia saeua puellae,
　　clauditur et dura ianua firma sera.
ianua difficilis domini, te uerberet imber,
　　te Iovis imperio fulmina missa petant.
ianua, iam pateas uni mihi, uicta querellis,
　　neu furtim uerso cardine aperta sones;　　　　　　10
et mala siqua tibi dixit dementia nostra,
　　ignoscas: capiti sint precor illa meo.
te meminisse decet quae plurima uoce peregi
　　supplice, cum posti florida serta darem.
tu quoque, ne timide custodes, Delia, falle;
　　audendum est: fortes adiuuat ipsa Venus.
illa fauet seu quis iuuenis noua limina temptat
　　seu reserat fixo dente puella fores;
illa docet furtim molli decedere lecto,
　　illa pedem nullo ponere posse sono,　　　　　　20
illa uiro coram nutus conferre loquaces
　　blandaque compositis abdere uerba notis.
nec docet hoc omnes sed quos nec inertia tardat
　　nec uetat obscura surgere nocte timor.
en ego cum tenebris tota uagor anxius urbe
　　. . .
nec sinit occurrat quisquam qui corpora ferro
　　uulneret aut rapta praemia ueste petat.
quisquis amore tenetur eat tutusque sacerque
　　qualibet; insidias non timuisse decet.　　　　　　30
non mihi pigra nocent hibernae frigora noctis,
　　non mihi cum multa decidit imber aqua;
non labor hic laedit, reseret modo Delia postes
　　et uocet ad digiti me taciturna sonum.

2

Pour more unwatered wine,* and let it overcome
    fresh grief so sleep controls my weary eyes
and, when my brow is Bacchus-bludgeoned,* may no man
    awaken me as barren passion rests.
My girl is now held hostage by a surly guard
    and her stout door is shut and bolted tight.
Tough husband's door, may you be pummelled by the rain
    and sought by lightning launched at Jove's command!
Door, open just for me, relenting to my pleas,
    and as the hinge turns slyly, make no sound,   10
and pardon me for cursing you while I was crazed;
    I ask you let that fall upon my head.
It's fitting you recall my vows and pleading tone
    as I hung wreaths of flowers on your frame.
Delia, you must indeed deceive the guard! Be daring!
    Venus* herself assists those who are bold!
She's guiding when a boy attempts an unknown entrance
    or a girl with hairpin* picks locked doors.
She shows them how to tiptoe from a downy bed,
    how, soundlessly, to put a foot on ground,   20
how, husband near, to change a heart with knowing nods
    and hide seductive words with preset signs.
She shows this not to all—just those unslowed by sloth
    and unafraid to rise in dark of night.
Look, when I'm tense and roaming through the city gloom,
    [Venus is there to make sure I am safe]
and do not meet a stranger who would slice my body
    with a knife or take my clothes as loot.
A person gripped by love should travel safe and blessed*
    where he may wish; no ambush should be feared.   30
The numbing chills of winter nights don't bother me,
    nor do the heavy showers drenching me.
No harm is done if Delia opens a locked door
    and softly calls me with a finger snap.

parcite luminibus, seu uir seu femina fiat
　　obuia: celari uult sua furta Venus.
neu strepitu terrete pedum neu quaerite nomen
　　neu prope fulgenti lumina ferte face.
siquis et imprudens aspexerit occulat ille
　　perque deos omnes se meminisse neget;　　　　　　　40
nam fuerit quicumque loquax, is sanguine natam
　　is Venerem e rabido sentiet esse mari.
nec tamen huic credet coniunx tuus, ut mihi uerax
　　pollicita est magico saga ministerio.
hanc ego de caelo ducentem sidera uidi;
　　fluminis haec rabido carmine uertit iter;
haec cantu finditque solum manesque sepulcris
　　elicit et tepido deuocat ossa rogo.
iam tenet infernas magico stridore cateruas;
　　iam iubet aspersas lacte referre pedem.　　　　　　50
cum libet, haec tristi depellit nubila caelo;
　　cum libet, aestiuo conuocat orbe niues.
sola tenere malas Medeae dicitur herbas,
　　sola feros Hecatae perdomuisse canes.
haec mihi composuit cantus quis fallere posses;
　　ter cane, ter dictis despue carminibus:
ille nihil poterit de nobis credere cuiquam,
　　non sibi, si in molli uiderit ipse toro.
tu tamen abstineas aliis, nam cetera cernet
　　omnia, de me uno sentiet ille nihil.　　　　　　　60
quid credam? nempe haec eadem se dixit amores
　　cantibus aut herbis soluere posse meos,
et me lustrauit taedis, et nocte serena
　　concidit ad magicos hostia pulla deos.
non ego totus abesset amor sed mutuus esset
　　orabam, nec te posse carere uelim.
ferreus ille fuit qui, te cum posset habere,
　　maluerit praedas stultus et arma sequi.
ille licet Cilicum uictas agat ante cateruas,
　　ponat et in capto Martia castra solo,　　　　　　70
totus et argento contectus totus et auro
　　insideat celeri conspiciendus equo,

Stop looking, whether you're a woman or a man
   approaching! Venus wants her thefts* concealed!
Don't terrorize with clomping feet! Don't ask our names!
   Don't carry flaming torches when nearby!
If someone sees by chance, then let him be discreet
   and swear by all the gods he 'can't recall'—   40
for if a person gossips, he will learn that Venus
   is the child of savage seas and blood,*
and yet your spouse will doubt it (as an honest witch*
   assured me through her mystic conjuring).
I've witnessed her seducing stars down from the sky;
   she turns a raging river with a spell.
Her chanting splits the earth, draws spirits from the grave,
   and summons bones from embers of the pyre.
First, she directs the demons with her mystic moans,
   then she commands retreat with sprinkled milk.   50
She chases clouds from gloomy skies when she desires;
   she calls down summer snow when she desires.
Only she has Medea's toxic herbs,* it's said;
   only she tamed fierce hounds of Hecate.*
She made a spell for me so that you can deceive.
   Chant it three times;* when finished, spit three times.
He* will not trust the tales of us—not even if
   his own eyes see us on a downy bed.
Still, shun all others, for he will observe the rest
   and I will be the only unseen one.   60
What? Should I trust her? She herself, of course, declared
   she could dispel my love with spells and herbs,
and cleansed me with a pine-torch; on a cloudless night
   she slew a dusky victim for dark gods.*
I wasn't praying love would end, but that it would
   be mutual, nor would I want to leave you.
That fool was iron who, when you were his to have,
   preferred instead pursuing war and plunder.
Let him repel Cilicia's defeated troops*
   still in his path and camp on captured ground!   70
Astride his speedy steed, completely sheathed in gold
   and silver, let him be a spectacle!

ipse boues mea si tecum modo Delia possim
    iungere et in solito pascere monte pecus;
et te dum liceat teneris retinere lacertis,
    mollis et inculta sit mihi somnus humo.
quid Tyrio recubare toro sine amore secundo
    prodest, cum fletu nox uigilanda uenit?
nam neque tum plumae nec stragula picta soporem
    nec sonitus placidae ducere possit aquae.   80
num Veneris magnae uiolaui numina uerbo
    et mea nunc poenas impia lingua luit?
num feror incestus sedes adiisse deorum
    sertaque de sanctis deripuisse focis?
non ego, si merui, dubitem procumbere templis
    et dare sacratis oscula liminibus,
non ego tellurem genibus perrepere supplex
    et miserum sancto tundere poste caput.
at tu qui lentus rides mala nostra caueto:
    mox tibi et iratus saeuiet usque deus.   90
uidi ego qui iuuenum miseros lusisset amores
    post Veneris uinclis subdere colla senem,
et sibi blanditias tremula componere uoce
    et manibus canas fingere uelle comas;
stare nec ante fores puduit caraeue puellae
    ancillam medio detinuisse foro.
hunc puer, hunc iuuenis turba circumterit arta,
    despuit in molles et sibi quisque sinus.
at mihi parce, Venus. semper tibi dedita seruit
    mens mea. quid messes uris acerba tuas?   100

My Delia, just to be with you, I'd yoke an ox
    and feed the sheep upon a humble hill
and, while allowed to hold you with my loving arms,
    I'd softly sleep upon the rugged ground!
What good is lying loveless on a bed from Tyre*
    when evening comes with tears and restlessness?
Because then neither feathers nor embroidered sheets
    nor water's lilting sounds* can lead to sleep.   80
Have I now snubbed almighty Venus with my words
    and so my godless tongue must pay the price?
Is it now rumoured I defiled the homes of gods
    and snatched some garland* from the holy altars?
If guilty, I'd not shrink from falling prone at shrines
    and pressing lips upon their blessed thresholds,
nor, as my penance, crawling on my knees through dirt
    and banging my sad head on sacred doorjambs!
But callous you, who mock my suffering, beware!
    A god won't punish the same man for long!   90
I've seen the man who mocked a youth's unhappy love
    then thrust his neck when old in chains of Venus,
and practise words of seduction with a shaky voice,
    and try to groom his greying hair by hand,
and never blush to stand before a girlfriend's door
    or stop her handmaid in the marketplace.*
Young men and boys surrounded him in swirling mobs,
    and each one spat on his own tender breast.*
But spare me, Venus! My devoted spirit keeps
    on serving you! Why let rage burn your harvest?   100

3

Ibitis Aegaeas sine me, Messalla, per undas,
    o utinam memores, ipse cohorsque, mei!
me tenet ignotis aegrum Phaeacia terris,
    abstineas auidas Mors precor atra manus.
abstineas, Mors atra, precor: non hic mihi mater
    quae legat in maestos ossa perusta sinus,
non soror Assyrios cineri quae dedat odores
    et fleat effusis ante sepulcra comis;
Delia non usquam, quae me quam mitteret urbe
    dicitur ante omnes consuluisse deos.   10
illa sacras pueri sortes ter sustulit: illi
    rettulit e trinis omina certa puer.
cuncta dabant reditus, tamen est deterrita numquam
    quin fleret nostras respiceretque uias.
ipse ego solator, cum iam mandata dedissem,
    quaerebam tardas anxius usque moras.
aut ego sum causatus aues aut omina dira
    Saturniue sacram me tenuisse diem.
o quotiens ingressus iter mihi tristia dixi
    offensum in porta signa dedisse pedem!   20
audeat inuito ne quis discedere amore
    aut sciet egressum se prohibente deo.
quid tua nunc Isis mihi, Delia, quid mihi prosunt
    illa tua totiens aera repulsa manu,
quidue, pie dum sacra colis, pureque lauari
    te (memini) et puro secubuisse toro?
nunc, dea, nunc succurre mihi, nam posse mederi
    picta docet templis multa tabella tuis,
ut mea uotiuas persoluens Delia uoces
    ante sacras lino tecta fores sedeat   30
bisque die resoluta comas tibi dicere laudes
    insignis turba debeat in Pharia.
at mihi contingat patrios celebrare Penates
    reddereque antiquo menstrua tura Lari.

3

Messalla, you will sail Aegean seas without me.
  O that your staff and you remember me!
Phaeacia* confines me, sick, in foreign lands;
  grim Death, please keep your greedy hand away!
Away, grim Death! I have no mother here to clutch
  my blackened bones beside her grieving breast,
no wild-haired sister dousing Syrian perfume
  upon my ash* and sobbing by my grave,
no Delia anywhere, who checked with all the gods,
  it's said, before she let me leave the city.   10
Three times* she drew a slaveboy's sacred lots;* the boy
  declared to her three times the signs were certain.
It all foretold return, but she was not deterred.
  Indeed, she wept and fussed about our journeys.
When I, her consolation, finished my farewells
  I tried to find some way to stall or wait.
My pretext would be birds or dire prophecies,
  or Saturn's holy day* was keeping me.
When footloose on the road, how often did I say
  my tripping at a gate portended grief?   20
Let no man dare abandon a reluctant love—
  or he will learn the trip's divinely banned!
Delia, what is your Isis* now to me? What good
  are those bronze rattles* you so often shook?
Or, while a pious follower, those cleansing baths
  and nights of abstinence* I can't forget?
Now, goddess, help me *now* (for many painted murals
  in your temples teach that you can heal)
so that, my Delia, honouring the vows she voiced,
  sits linen-clad* outside your sacred gate   30
and, with unbound hair,* twice each day* repeats the praise
  on show among Pharian multitudes—*
but let *me* worship the Penates* of my house
  and offer ancient Lares monthly incense.

quam bene Saturno uiuebant rege, priusquam
    tellus in longas est patefacta uias!
nondum caeruleas pinus contempserat undas
    effusum uentis praebueratque sinum;
nec uagus ignotis repetens compendia terris
    presserat externa nauita merce ratem.   40
illo non ualidus subiit iuga tempore taurus,
    non domito frenos ore momordit equus;
non domus ulla fores habuit, non fixus in agris
    qui regeret certis finibus arua lapis;
ipsae mella dabant quercus, ultroque ferebant
    obuia securis ubera lactis oues;
non acies non ira fuit non bella nec ensem
    immiti saeuus duxerat arte faber.
nunc Ioue sub domino caedes et uulnera semper,
    nunc mare, nunc leti mille repente uiae.   50
parce, pater: timidum non me periuria terrent,
    non dicta in sanctos impia uerba deos.
quod si fatales iam nunc expleuimus annos,
    fac lapis inscriptis stet super ossa notis:
HIC IACET IMMITI CONSVMPTVS MORTE TIBVLLVS
    MESSALLAM TERRA DVM SEQVITVRQVE MARI.
sed me, quod facilis tenero sum semper amori,
    ipsa Venus campos ducet in Elysios.
hic choreae cantusque uigent, passimque uagantes
    dulce sonant tenui gutture carmen aues;   60
fert casiam non culta seges totosque per agros
    floret odoratis terra benigna rosis:
ac iuuenum series teneris immixta puellis
    ludit et assidue proelia miscet Amor.
illic est cuicumque rapax mors uenit amanti,
    et gerit insigni myrtea serta coma.
at scelerata iacet sedes in nocte profunda
    abdita, quam circum flumina nigra sonant,
Tisiphoneque impexa feros pro crinibus angues
    saeuit et huc illuc inpia turba fugit;   70
tunc niger in porta serpentum Cerberus ore
    stridet et aeratas excubat ante fores.

How wonderful the living was in Saturn's reign*
    before the world was opened by long roads!
Pine masts had not yet learned to scorn blue ocean waves
    or give the wind their puffed-out chests of sails,
nor had the roaming sailors crowded rough-hewn boats
    for gains on imports from exotic lands.   40
In olden days no sturdy bull would take the yoke,
    no horse was tamed to chew upon a bit.
The houses had no doors, nor were there stones on fields
    that fixed the boundaries of men's estates.
The oaks themselves bore honey, and ewes freely offered
    udders full of milk to carefree men.
There were no feuds, no wars, no armies, nor swords forged
    by brutal crafting of a callous blacksmith.
With Jove now lord* there's constant gore and slaughter, now
    there's sea, now sudden death by endless ways.   50
Father, show mercy. I'm not frightened by false oaths,
    nor by impious slights* of sacred gods,
and so if I have now consumed my destined years,
    set stone above my bones with this inscription:
HERE LIES TIBULLUS, WORN AWAY BY BITTER DEATH
SERVING MESSALLA ON THE LAND AND SEA.*
Since, though, I've always been a mark for gentle Love,
    Venus will lead me to Elysian fields.*
There songs and dances flourish, and from slender throats
    the restless birds produce a gentle song.   60
Untilled land sprouts with cinnamon,* and in the fields
    the fragrant roses bloom in fertile soil,
and lines of youthful men and tender girls cavort,
    and Love is joining the incessant battle.
Lovers for whom rapacious Death has come are there,
    and sport their special myrtle in their tresses,*
but lost in boundless night, the Seat of Evil* lies
    surrounded by the roar of murky rivers.
With her wild writhing snakes for hair, Tisiphone*
    erupts and godless mobs flee everywhere,   70
then snake-mouthed Cerberus,* in gloom around the gate,
    hisses and stands his watch before bronze doors.

illic Iunonem temptare Ixionis ausi
  uersantur celeri noxia membra rota,
porrectusque nouem Tityos per iugera terrae
  assiduas atro uiscere pascit aues.
Tantalus est illic et circum stagna sed acrem
  iam iam poturi deserit unda sitim;
et Danai proles, Veneris quod numina laesit,
  in caua Lethaeas dolia portat aquas.   80
illic sit quicumque meos uiolauit amores,
  optauit lentas et mihi militias.
at tu casta, precor, maneas sanctique pudoris
  assideat custos sedula semper anus.
haec tibi fabellas referat positaque lucerna
  deducat plena stamina longa colu,
ac circum, grauibus pensis affixa, puella
  paulatim somno fessa remittat opus.
tunc ueniam subito nec quisquam nuntiet ante
  sed uidear caelo missus adesse tibi.   90
tunc mihi qualis eris, longos turbata capillos,
  obuia nudato, Delia, curre pede.
hoc precor: hunc illum nobis Aurora nitentem
  Luciferum roseis candida portet equis.

There's Ixion,* who dared attempting Juno's rape;
    his guilty limbs are whirling in the wheel,
and stretched across nine acres there is Tityos;*
    his bloody organs feed relentless birds.
There's Tantalus* with water near, though waves recede
    as he attempts to quench his bitter thirst.
And, since they slighted Venus, the daughters of Danaus*
    haul Lethe's waters into leaking vats.   80
May that place be for those who have defiled my love
    and wished for me a leisurely campaign!
But stay chaste, I implore you! May your ancient nurse
    remain by you and guard your modesty!
May she retell old tales for you and pull long threads
    from her full spindles when the lamp is set down,
though all around her girls intent on mounds of wool
    are slowing down and nodding off at work.
Then I will burst in, unannounced by anyone
    (but may I seem divinely sent to you),   90
and then, just as you are, with long dishevelled hair,
    come running, Delia, with bare feet to meet me.
For this I pray: may bright Aurora bring to us
    the brilliant morning star on rosy steeds.

4

'Sic umbrosa tibi contingant tecta, Priape,
    ne capiti soles ne noceantque niues:
quae tua formosos cepit sollertia? certe
    non tibi barba nitet, non tibi culta coma est;
nudus et hibernae producis frigora brumae,
    nudus et aestiui tempora sicca Canis.'
sic ego. tunc Bacchi respondit rustica proles,
    armatus curua, sic mihi, falce deus:
'o fuge te tenerae puerorum credere turbae,
    nam causam iusti semper amoris habent.   10
hic placet angustis quod equum compescit habenis;
    hic placidam niueo pectore pellit aquam.
hic quia fortis adest audacia cepit, at illi
    uirgineus teneras stat pudor ante genas.
sed ne te capiant, primo si forte negabit,
    taedia: paulatim sub iuga colla dabit.
longa dies homini docuit parere leones;
    longa dies molli saxa peredit aqua.
annus in apricis maturat collibus uuas;
    annus agit certa lucida signa uice.   20
nec iurare time: Veneris periuria uenti
    irrita per terras et freta summa ferunt.
gratia magna Ioui: uetuit pater ipse ualere
    iurasset cupide quicquid ineptus amor;
perque suas impune sinit Dictynna sagittas
    affirmes crines perque Minerua suos.
at si tardus eris errabis. transiet aetas
    quam cito: non segnis stat remeatue dies.
quam cito purpureos deperdit terra colores,
    quam cito formosas populus alta comas;   30
quam iacet, infirmae uenere ubi fata senectae,
    qui prior Eleo est carcere missus equus.
uidi iam iuuenem premeret cum serior aetas
    maerentem stultos praeteriisse dies.

4

'Priapus,* so a shady cover may be yours
    and neither sun nor snowfall harm your head,
how does your guile enthrall the gorgeous boys? For sure,
    your beard is short on shine, your hair's a mess,
and, naked, you extend the winter solstice chills
    and, naked, the dry times of Dog Star* summers.'
That's what I said. Then Bacchus' bucolic child,*
    the god who's armed with curving scythe, replied:
'O flee! Don't trust yourself with throngs of callow boys,
    for they will always offer grounds for love.   10
One thrills by tightly reining in a horse; some other
    beats still water with his snowy breast.
This one transfixes with his bold panache—that one
    with tender cheeks that keep their virgin blush.
He will refuse at first, but don't become worn down!
    His neck will bit by bit accept a yoke.
Long days have taught the lions to submit to man.
    Long days let gentle water eat through rock.
A year in sunshine ripens grapes upon the hills;
    a year revolves bright stars on settled routes.   20
Don't shy from making vows! Across tall straits and lands,
    the winds transport the broken oaths of love.
Great thanks to Jove! The Father has himself forbidden
    whatever silly love has sworn in lust,
and one can break vows by Dictynna's* arrows or
    Minerva's* tresses with no retribution.
But if you're slow, you shall be lost! How fast the time
    escapes—the days don't linger or return!
How fast the Earth relinquishes its purple hues!
    How fast tall poplars lose their gorgeous leaves!   30
How, when frail age becomes its fate, a horse who once
    would bolt from gates at Elis* stumbles down.
I have already seen a youth depressed by growing old
    lamenting folly in the days gone by.

crudeles diui. serpens nouus exuit annos;
   formae non ullam Fata dedere moram.
solis aeterna est Baccho Phoeboque iuuentas,
   nam decet intonsus crinis utrumque deum.
tu puero quodcumque tuo temptare libebit
   cedas: obsequio plurima uincet amor.   40
neu comes ire neges quamuis uia longa paretur
   et Canis arenti torreat arua siti,
quamuis praetexens picta ferrugine caelum
   uenturam admittat nubifer arcus aquam.
uel si caeruleas puppi uolet ire per undas,
   ipse leuem remo per freta pelle ratem.
nec te paeniteat duros subiisse labores
   aut opera insuetas atteruisse manus.
nec, uelit insidiis altas si claudere ualles,
   dum placeas, umeri retia ferre negent.   50
si uolet arma, leui temptabis ludere dextra;
   saepe dabis nudum, uincat ut ille, latus.
tunc tibi mitis erit, rapias tunc cara licebit
   oscula: pugnabit sed tibi rapta dabit.
rapta dabit primo, post afferet ipse roganti,
   post etiam collo se implicuisse uelit.
heu male nunc artes miseras haec saecula tractant!
   iam tener assueuit munera uelle puer.
at tu, qui Venerem docuisti uendere primus,
   quisquis es, infelix urgeat ossa lapis.   60
Pieridas, pueri, doctos et amate poetas,
   aurea nec superent munera Pieridas.
carmine purpurea est Nisi coma; carmina ni sint,
   ex umero Pelopis non nituisset ebur.
quem referent Musae, uiuet, dum robora tellus
   dum caelum stellas dum uehet amnis aquas.
at qui non audit Musas, qui uendit amorem,
   Idaeae currus ille sequatur Opis
et ter centenas erroribus expleat urbes
   et secet ad Phrygios uilia membra modos.   70
blanditiis uult esse locum Venus: illa querellis
   supplicibus, miseris fletibus illa fauet.'

Cruel gods! A serpent sloughs off years, and is renewed.
   The Fates aren't granting any breaks for looks.
Only Phoebus and Bacchus* have eternal youth
   since long and uncut hair befits both gods.
Just yield to anything your lad desires you
   to try; love wins most by subservience.   40
Don't spurn a trip as friends, although the road seems lengthy
   and the Dogstar burns dry fields with drought,
although a cloud-drenched rainbow is absorbing water
   as the sky is fringed with shades of violet.
If he likes being on a boat amid blue waves,
   then row the skiff across the waves yourself,
and you should not regret hard labours you endured
   or wearing out your unused hands with work.
To please him, if he wants to seal a high-walled valley,
   don't refuse to lug the hunting nets.   50
If he wants war, try playing with a gentle hand;
   keep your flank exposed so he will win.
Then he'll be kind to you—he'll let a cherished kiss
   be snatched; he'll fight, but give you what was snatched.
He gives what's taken first, then brings himself when asked,
   then even wants himself draped on your neck.
Alas, today this age mishandles wretched arts;
   now tender boys have learned to grasp for gifts,
while you, whoever you may be, who first taught whoring,
   may an ill-timed tombstone crush your bones!   60
Boys, you must love the Muses and the learned poets!
   Don't elevate gold gifts above the Muses!
With verse it's purple hair for Nisus;* without verse,
   ivory would not have shone from Pelops'* shoulder.
Someone the Muses name will live while land has oaks,
   while skies have stars, while rivers flow with water,
but one deaf to the Muses, and who sells his love,
   shall trail the chariot of Ops of Ida,*
and let him wander through three hundred towns while lost
   and hack vile parts to beats of Phrygia!*   70
Venus herself leaves room for flattery; she favours
   wretched sobs and pleas from suppliants.'

haec mihi quae canerem Titio deus edidit ore,
  sed Titium coniunx haec meminisse uetat.
pareat ille suae: uos me celebrate magistrum
  quos male habet multa callidus arte puer.
gloria cuique sua est: me qui spernentur amantes
  consultent; cunctis ianua nostra patet.
tempus erit cum me Veneris praecepta ferentem
  deducat iuuenum sedula turba senem.   80
eheu, quam Marathus lento me torquet amore!
  deficiunt artes, deficiuntque doli.
parce, puer, quaeso, ne turpis fabula fiam
  cum mea ridebunt uana magisteria.

This the god spoke so I would sing to Titius*
    (although his wife demands that he forget).
Let him obey his wife! May those deceived by tricks
    of cunning lads proclaim me as the expert!
To each his source of pride! For me it's counselling
    spurned lovers. For them all, my door is open.
Someday a zealous youthful mob will dote on me,
    the greybeard bearing principles of love.   80
Alas, Marathus slowly tortures me with love!
    Deception fails and sly manoeuvres fail.
Please spare me, boy, so I won't be a shameful joke
    when people laugh at pointless expertise!

5

Asper eram et bene discidium me ferre loquebar,
    at mihi nunc longe gloria fortis abest;
namque agor ut per plana citus sola uerbere turben
    quem celer assueta uersat ab arte puer.
ure ferum et torque, libeat ne dicere quicquam
    magnificum posthac: horrida uerba doma.
parce tamen per te furtiui foedera lecti
    per Venerem quaeso conpositumque caput.
ille ego, cum tristi morbo defessa iaceres,
    te dicor uotis eripuisse meis.   10
ipseque te circum lustraui sulpure puro,
    carmine cum magico praecinuisset anus.
ipse procuraui ne possent saeua nocere
    somnia ter sancta deueneranda mola.
ipse ego, uelatus filo tunicisque solutis,
    uota nouem Triuiae nocte silente dedi.
omnia persolui: fruitur nunc alter amore,
    et precibus felix utitur ille meis.
at mihi felicem uitam, si salua fuisses,
    fingebam demens, sed renuente deo: 20
'rura colam, frugumque aderit mea Delia custos,
    area dum messes sole calente teret;
aut mihi seruabit plenis in lintribus uuas
    pressaque ueloci candida musta pede.
consuescet numerare pecus; consuescet amantis
    garrulus in dominae ludere uerna sinu.
illa deo sciet agricolae pro uitibus uuam,
    pro segete spicas, pro grege ferre dapem.
illa regat cunctos, illi sint omnia curae,
    at iuuet in tota me nihil esse domo.   30
huc ueniet Messalla meus, cui dulcia poma
    Delia selectis detrahat arboribus,
et tantum uenerata uirum, hunc sedula curet,
    huic paret atque epulas ipsa ministra gerat.'

5

I claimed I took the break-up well, and I was tough,
    but my persistent pride is now long gone,
since, like a top with string, I move on level ground
    while whirled by talents of a skilful lad.
Torture and brand the beast* so he no longer brags
    of anything else! Tame his savage speech,
but spare me, I request, by secret bedroom bonds,
    by Venus and the head conjoined with mine!*
I'm told I snatched you from disaster with my prayers
    as you were lying worn out by disease   10
and I myself spread cleansing sulphur close to you
    once some hag had intoned a magic spell.
For your protection I warded nightmares off
    by offering the sacred grain three times.*
I vowed nine times to Trivia in still of night
    dressed in a loosened tunic and wool cord.
I honoured them all. Now another lucky man
    enjoys my love and profits from my prayers,
yet I would dream (while crazy) of my happy life
    if you recovered, but the god refused.*   20
I'd plough the farmland while my Delia guards the yields
    that grind on threshing floors in blazing sun,
or she would oversee the grapes in bulging troughs
    and white wine just pressed by speedy feet.
She'd know a cattle count; a chatty servant boy*
    would frolic on her loving lady's lap.
She'd learn gifts for the god of farmers:* grapes for vines;
    cornstalks for cornfields; feasting for a flock.
She'd manage everyone and care for everything
    while I'd love being nothing in the house.   30
When my Messalla* visits, Delia would then pick
    for him sweet apples from the choicest trees,
and, honouring such greatness, she would work with zeal,
    and make and serve the meal, with her the servant.

haec mihi fingebam quae nunc Eurusque Notusque
    iactat odoratos uota per Armenios.
saepe ego temptaui curas depellere uino
    at dolor in lacrimas uerterat omne merum.
saepe aliam tenui sed iam cum gaudia adirem
    admonuit dominae deseruitque Venus.   40
tunc me discedens deuotum femina dixit,
    et pudet, et narrat scire nefanda meam.
non facit hoc uerbis: facie tenerisque lacertis
    deuouet et flauis nostra puella comis.
talis ad Haemonium Nereis Pelea quondam
    uecta est frenato caerula pisce Thetis.
haec nocuere mihi quod adest huic diues amator.
    uenit in exitium callida lena meum.
sanguineas edat illa dapes atque ore cruento
    tristia cum multo pocula felle bibat.   50
hanc uolitent animae circum sua fata querentes
    semper et e tectis strix uiolenta canat.
ipsa fame stimulante furens herbasque sepulcris
    quaerat et a saeuis ossa relicta lupis;
currat et inguinibus nudis ululetque per urbem,
    post agat e triuiis aspera turba canum.
eueniet: dat signa deus. sunt numina amanti,
    saeuit et iniusta lege relicta Venus.
at tu quam primum sagae praecepta rapacis
    desere, nam donis uincitur omnis amor.   60
pauper erit praesto semper tibi, pauper adibit
    primus et in tenero fixus erit latere.
pauper in angusto fidus comes agmine turbae
    subicietque manus efficietque uiam.
pauper ad occultos furtim deducet amicos
    uinclaque de niueo detrahet ipse pede.
heu canimus frustra nec uerbis uicta patescit
    ianua sed plena est percutienda manu.
at tu qui potior nunc es mea fata timeto:
    uersatur celeri fors leuis orbe rotae.   70
non frustra quidam iam nunc in limine perstat
    sedulus ac crebro prospicit ac refugit

This was my dream: vows scattered now by winds from east
    and west across perfumed Armenia.*
I've often tried to banish pains of love with wine,
    but sorrow turned the uncut wine to tears.
I've often held another, but when I near joy,
    Venus evokes my mistress and departs,   40
then, as she left, the woman said that I was hexed
    (O shame!) and claimed my girlfriend knew black arts.
This isn't done with words because my girl enchants
    with beauty, tender arms and golden hair
like Thetis,* blue-eyed Nereid, whom bridled fish
    once bore to Peleus of Thessaly.
This brings me pain, for with a wealthy suitor near,*
    the sneaky madam comes for my destruction.
May she consume* a feast of blood with bloodstained lips
    and drink a bitter goblet full of gall!   50
May spirits fly around her, moaning of their fate,
    and may an owl* keep screeching from the roof,
and, hunger-wracked and raging, may she scour graves
    for weeds and bones abandoned by fierce wolves,
and run and shriek through town with crotch exposed as packs
    of angry dogs expel her from the crossroads!*
'So be it,' some god signals.* Lovers have their gods
    and Venus rants when left with unjust law.
But you must spurn the greedy hag's advice right now!
    Must every passion be undone by bribes?   60
A poor man clings to you. A poor man draws near first
    and will remain along your tender side.
A poor man—the good friend when jammed into a crowd—
    will lift you with his hands and get you through.
A poor man will escort you to your secret friends
    and take the sandals off your snowy feet.
Alas, I sing in vain; one can't persuade shut doors,*
    but one must beat them down with cash in hand,
though you, who are supreme now, you should fear my fate;
    the fickle wheel of Fortune* quickly turns.   70
It's not in vain that someone's at her entrance now;
    intense and quick, he checks it out and flees,

	et simulat transire domum, mox deinde recurrit,
		solus et ante ipsas excreat usque fores.
	nescioquid furtiuus Amor parat. utere, quaeso,
		dum licet: in liquida nat tibi linter aqua.

and then pretends to pass the house, then soon returns
  alone and keeps on coughing by those doors.
Sly Love prepares some scheme. I ask you, while you can,
  to revel; your small vessel drifts on current.*

6

Semper ut inducar blandos offers mihi uultus,
    post tamen es misero tristis et asper, Amor.
quid tibi saeuitiae mecum est? an gloria magna est
    insidias homini composuisse deum?
nam mihi tenduntur casses. iam Delia furtim
    nescioquem tacita callida nocte fouet.
illa quidem tam multa negat, sed credere durum est;
    sic etiam de me pernegat usque uiro.
ipse miser docui quo posset ludere pacto
    custodes: eheu nunc premor arte mea.   10
fingere tunc didicit causas ut sola cubaret,
    cardine tunc tacito uertere posse fores.
tunc sucos herbasque dedi quis liuor abiret
    quem facit impresso mutua dente Venus.
at tu, fallacis coniunx incaute puellae,
    me quoque seruato peccet ut illa nihil.
neu iuuenes celebret multo sermone caueto,
    neue cubet laxo pectus aperta sinu,
neu te decipiat nutu, digitoque liquorem
    ne trahat et mensae ducat in orbe notas.   20
exibit quam saepe, time, seu uisere dicet
    sacra Bonae maribus non adeunda Deae.
at mihi si credas, illam sequar unus ad aras;
    tunc mihi non oculis sit timuisse meis.
saepe uelut gemmas eius signumque probarem
    per causam memini me tetigisse manum.
saepe mero somnum peperi tibi, at ipse bibebam
    sobria supposita pocula uictor aqua.
non ego te laesi prudens; ignosce fatenti.
    iussit Amor; contra quis ferat arma deos?   30
ille ego sum (nec me iam dicere uera pudebit)
    instabat tota cui tua nocte canis.
quid tenera tibi coniuge opus, tua si bona nescis
    seruare? frustra clauis inest foribus.

6

You always flatter me, Love, so I'm snared, though later,
    to my sorrow, you are harsh and sad.
Why are you cruel to me? Or is there special glory
    when a god has set a human trap?
Once more your nets* are spread for me. Now, this still night,
    sly Delia's* warming someone* undercover.
She swears it isn't true, but trust is hard in light
    of how she still denies me to her 'husband'.*
Wretch that I am, I taught her how to fool the guards!
    Alas, I'm being squeezed now by my tricks!   10
She learned to make up reasons she should sleep alone
    and how to turn a hinge without a sound,
and then I gave her herbs and potions that erase
    the marks of passion left behind by teeth.
But you, incautious 'husband' of a cheating girl,
    should guard against me too so she won't sin!
Take care that she not visit with young men for talk,
    nor dine unfastened with her breast exposed,
nor fool you with a nod, nor trace a circle on
    the table with her drink to send a signal.*   20
Fret if she's often out or says she's off to see
    Good Goddess* rites that men must not attend,
but trust me, and I'll come alone to the altars;
    would then have no fear about my eyes.*
As cover I would often check her gems and seal
    just, I remember, to have held her hand.
Strong wine would often bring you sleep, though I, the victor,*
    traded it for cups of sober water.
I didn't mean you harm! Forgive what was confessed!
    Love was in charge (and who can fight a god?).   30
I will not blush to speak the truth, for it was me
    at whom your dog was barking all night long!
What value is your gentle 'wife'?* If you don't know
    to guard your goods, your door-key turns in vain!

te tenet, absentes alios suspirat amores
   et simulat subito condoluisse caput.
at mihi seruandam credas: non saeua recuso
   uerbera, detrecto non ego uincla pedum.
tunc procul absitis, quisquis colit arte capillos
   et fluit effuso cui toga laxa sinu;   40
quisquis et occurret, ne possit crimen habere
   stet procul aut alia transeat ille uia.
sic fieri iubet ipse deus, sic magna sacerdos
   est mihi diuino uaticinata sono.
haec, ubi Bellonae motu est agitata, nec acrem
   flammam, non amens uerbera torta timet.
ipsa bipenne suos caedit uiolenta lacertos
   sanguineque effuso spargit inulta deam,
statque latus praefixa ueru, stat saucia pectus,
   et canit euentus quos dea magna monet: 50
'parcite quam custodit Amor uiolare puellam,
   ne pigeat magno post tetigisse malo.
attigerit, labentur opes, ut uulnere nostro
   sanguis, ut hic uentis diripiturque cinis.'
et tibi nescio quas dixit, mea Delia, poenas;
   si tamen admittas, sit precor illa leuis.
non ego te propter parco tibi, sed tua mater
   me mouet atque iras aurea uincit anus.
haec mihi te adducit tenebris multoque timore
   coniungit nostras clam taciturna manus.   60
haec foribusque manet noctu me affixa proculque
   cognoscit strepitus me ueniente pedum.
uiue diu mihi, dulcis anus: proprios ego tecum,
   sit modo fas, annos contribuisse uelim.
te semper natamque tuam te propter amabo:
   quicquid agit, sanguis est tamen illa tuus.
sit modo casta doce, quamuis non uitta ligatos
   impediat crines nec stola longa pedes.
et mihi sint durae leges, laudare nec ullam
   possim ego quin oculos appetat illa meos;   70
et, siquid peccasse putet, ducarque capillis
   immerito pronas proripiarque uias.

She holds you, sighs for someone who is an absent love,
    and suddenly pretends her head is aching,
but trust *me* with protecting her—I do not shirk
    cruel stripes or take the shackles* off my feet.
Then get out, those of you who coif your hair with skill
    and those whose togas hang with spacious folds,*   40
and let all those we meet, so they can not be blamed,
    remain apart or take another road!*
A god himself* so ordered; so a mighty priestess
    prophesied for me in godlike tones.
She, when Bellona's* palsies quake, is not afraid
    of glowing flames or twisting, frantic whips.
Using a two-edged axe, she wildly cuts her arms
    and, unharmed, spatters blood upon the goddess,
and, skewered on her side, she stands with wounded breast
    and chants predictions that the goddess prompts: 50
'Don't violate the girl whom Love is keeping safe
    so later it won't gall that you have sinned!
If someone touches her, his wealth shall drain—like blood
    out of my wounds, like ashes strewn by wind!'
For you, my Delia, she proposed some punishments,
    though if you're guilty,* I would plead for mercy.
It's not for you I spare you, but your mother moves me,
    and the old golden lady conquers rage.*
She leads you out to me in gloom while terrified
    and joins our hands covertly in the silence,   60
and she stays glued beside the doors at night and knows
    the noises made by my approaching feet.*
Live long, you sweet old woman! If it could be done
    between us two, I'd give you my own years.
I'll always love you and your daughter due to you.
    Whatever she may do, she's still your blood.
Just teach her to be chaste, although no headband cloaks
    her tresses nor a floor-length robe her feet.*
And there should be tough rules for me: I'd praise no other
    woman so she won't attack my eyes,   70
and if she *thinks* I've strayed, then she can grab my hair
    and drag me guiltless down the sloping streets!

non ego te pulsare uelim, sed uenerit iste
   si furor, optarim non habuisse manus.
nec saeuo sis casta metu sed mente fideli;
   mutuus absenti te mihi seruet amor.
at quae fida fuit nulli, post uicta senecta
   ducit inops tremula stamina torta manu,
firmaque conductis adnectit licia telis,
   tractaque de niueo uellere ducta putat.   80
hanc animo gaudente uident iuuenumque cateruae
   commemorant merito tot mala ferre senem.
hanc Venus ex alto flentem sublimis Olympo
   spectat et infidis quam sit acerba monet.
haec aliis maledicta cadant. nos, Delia, amoris
   exemplum cana simus uterque coma.

I'd never want to hit you, but if madness such
    as that did come, I'd pray to have no hands.
Do not be chaste from fear, but from a faithful heart.
    May mutual love guard you in my absence.
But when she's crushed by age, she who is true to none
    threads twisted yarn with weak and shaky hands,
and firmly ties the leashes to the rented loom,*
    and scours yarn obtained from snowy fleece,   80
and groups of youthful men observe with glee, and think
    it right she bears this hardship in old age.
From high Olympus Venus looks upon her tears
    and warns how harsh she is with faithless people.
Let curses like these fall on others! Let us be,
    Delia, the model of two white-haired lovers!*

7

Hunc cecinere diem Parcae, fatalia nentes
    stamina non ulli dissoluenda deo,
hunc fore Aquitanas posset qui fundere gentes,
    quem tremeret forti milite uictus Atur.
euenere: nouos pubes Romana triumphos
    uidit et euinctos bracchia capta duces;
at te uictrices lauros, Messalla, gerentem
    portabat nitidis currus eburnus equis.
non sine me est tibi partus honos: Tarbella Pyrene
    testis et Oceani litora Santonici,   10
testis Arar Rhodanusque celer magnusque Garunna,
    Carnutis et flaui caerula lympha Liger.
an te, Cydne, canam, tacitis qui leniter undis
    caeruleus placidis per uada serpis aquis?
quantus et aetherio contingens uertice nubes
    frigidus intonsos Taurus alat Cilicas?
quid referam ut uolitet crebras intacta per urbes
    alba Palaestino sancta columba Syro?
utque maris uastum prospectet turribus aequor
    prima ratem uentis credere docta Tyros?   20
qualis et, arentes cum findit Sirius agros,
    fertilis aestiua Nilus abundet aqua?
Nile pater, quanam possim te dicere causa
    aut quibus in terris occuluisse caput?
te propter nullos tellus tua postulat imbres,
    arida nec pluuio supplicat herba Ioui.
te canit atque suum pubes miratur Osirim
    barbara, Memphitem plangere docta bouem.
primus aratra manu sollerti fecit Osiris
    et teneram ferro sollicitauit humum.   30
primus inexpertae commisit semina terrae
    pomaque non notis legit ab arboribus.
hic docuit teneram palis adiungere uitem,
    hic uiridem dura caedere falce comam.

7

While spinning threads of fate a god cannot unwind,
    the Parcae* prophesied about this day,
this one that would disperse the tribes of Aquitaine,*
    that made the bravely conquered Atur* tremble.
So it has happened. Roman youths have seen new triumphs
    and the shackled arms of captured leaders,
and you, Messalla, wearing victor's laurels in
    a gleaming horse-drawn ivory chariot.*
You won no prize without me;* Santonican shores*
    and the Tarbelli's Pyrenees* are proof,   10
proof is Arar, the swift Rhodanus, great Garunna,
    crystal Liger* of the blond Carnutes.*
Or, Cydnus,* shall I sing of you whose silent waves
    skim azure waters of the placid shoals?
and how cold Taurus* feeds unshorn Cilicians
    by lifting his high crown up to the clouds?
Must I still say white doves revered by Syrians*
    fly safely through the towns of Palestine?
and, how Tyre*, first to trust the wind to guide its boats,
    scans vast expanses of the sea from towers?   20
And how, when Sirius* is parching drying fields
    in summertime, the fertile Nile is cresting?
What is the reason, Father Nile, and in what lands
    may I declare you hid your head from sight?*
Because of you your farmland never pleads for showers,
    no dry plant implores rain-giving Jove.
Young men from elsewhere taught to mourn the Memphis Bull*
    extol and honour you as their Osiris.
With skilful hands Osiris first produced the plough
    and then disturbed the virgin soil with iron.   30
He first committed seed to undeveloped land
    and gathered fruit from unfamiliar trees.
He taught the way to tie a tender vine to poles,
    the way to cut lush leaves with sturdy blades.

illi iucundos primum matura sapores
 expressa incultis uua dedit pedibus.
ille liquor docuit uoces inflectere cantu,
 mouit et ad certos nescia membra modos.
Bacchus et agricolae magno confecta labore
 pectora laetitiae dissoluenda dedit.   40
Bacchus et afflictis requiem mortalibus affert,
 crura licet dura conpede pulsa sonent.
non tibi sunt tristes curae nec luctus, Osiri,
 sed chorus et cantus et leuis aptus amor,
sed uarii flores et frons redimita corymbis,
 fusa sed ad teneros lutea palla pedes
et Tyriae uestes et dulcis tibia cantu
 et leuis occultis conscia cista sacris.
huc ades et Genium ludis Geniumque choreis
 concelebra et multo tempora funde mero. 50
illius et nitido stillent unguenta capillo,
 et capite et collo mollia serta gerat.
sic uenias, hodierne: tibi dem turis honores,
 liba et Mopsopio dulcia melle feram.
at tibi succrescat proles, quae facta parentis
 augeat et circum stet ueneranda senem.
nec taceat monumenta uiae quem Tuscula tellus
 candidaque antiquo detinet Alba Lare.
namque opibus congesta tuis hic glarea dura
 sternitur, hic apta iungitur arte silex.   60
te canat agricola a magna cum uenerit urbe
 serus inoffensum rettuleritque pedem.
at tu, Natalis, multos celebrande per annos,
 candidior semper candidiorque ueni.

For him ripe grapes in clusters squeezed by shoeless feet
   would first surrender their delightful flavours.
That liquor taught their voices modulated song
   and moved their untaught limbs in settled rhythms,*
and Bacchus, when a farmer finishes hard work,
   provides that joy is freed within his heart,   40
and Bacchus brings relief to mortals in distress
   though sturdy shackles* clank upon their legs.
Osiris, there are no concerns or woes with you,
   just dance and song and uncommitted love,
just coloured flowers coiled on heads and ivy strands,
   and golden robes* surrounding tender feet,
and finery from Tyre,* and sweet songs for flutes,
   and light reed baskets holding sacred secrets.*
Come join the games and dances for his Genius,*
   and honour his drenched brow with ample wine,   50
and let the ointment trickle off his gleaming hair,
   and let soft garlands drape his head and neck.
So come today; I'll honour you with frankincense
   and bring Mopsopian sweet honeycakes,*
but may your heirs* mature to build your legacy
   and stand by you in honour as you age,
and no one fail to praise your landmark road* in fields
   of Tusculum and Alba's old white homes,*
since there, built at your cost, packed gravel was laid down,
   there rock was tightly joined with fitting skill.*   60
When he is coming back from Rome late, may the farmer
   praise you and return without a stumble,
but you, Birth-Spirit,* celebrated through the years,
   come always brighter—and then brighter still!

8

Non ego celari possum quid nutus amantis
    quidue ferant miti lenia uerba sono,
nec mihi sunt sortes nec conscia fibra deorum,
    praecinit euentus nec mihi cantus auis:
ipsa Venus magico religatum bracchia nodo
    perdocuit, multis non sine uerberibus.
desine dissimulare: deus crudelius urit
    quos uidet inuitos succubuisse sibi.
quid tibi nunc molles prodest coluisse capillos
    saepeque mutatas disposuisse comas,   10
quid fuco splendente genas ornare, quid ungues
    artificis docta subsecuisse manu?
frustra iam uestes frustra mutantur amictus
    ansaque compressos colligat arta pedes.
illa placet, quamuis inculto uenerit ore
    nec nitidum tarda compserit arte caput.
num te carminibus num te pallentibus herbis
    deuouit tacito tempore noctis anus?
cantus uicinis fruges traducit ab agris,
    cantus et iratae detinet anguis iter,   20
cantus et e curru Lunam deducere temptat,
    et faceret si non aera repulsa sonent.
quid queror heu misero carmen nocuisse, quid herbas?
    forma nihil magicis utitur auxiliis;
sed corpus tetigisse nocet sed longa dedisse
    oscula sed femori conseruisse femur.
nec tu difficilis puero tamen esse memento;
    persequitur poenis tristia facta Venus.
munera nec poscas; det munera canus amator
    ut foueat molli frigida membra sinu.   30
carior est auro iuuenis cui leuia fulgent
    ora nec amplexus aspera barba terit.
huic tu candentes umero suppone lacertos
    et regum magnae despiciantur opes.

8

There is no hiding from me what some tender words
    in whispers and a lover's nod convey.
For me there are no lots, no livers linked to gods,
    no songbirds* that predict events for me.
Venus herself restrained my arms with magic knots;
    she taught me much (though not without some floggings).*
Don't hide your thoughts! A god* more fiercely scorches those
    he sees aren't willing to submit to him.
Now what's the point of beautifying your soft hair
    and always changing how it is arranged?   10
What do you get from dolling up with gleaming blush?
    What from shrewd artisans who clipped your nails?
In vain the robes keep changing—then in vain the cloaks—
    and laces tightly squeeze your narrow feet.
That girl can please, though she arrives with lips undone
    and spends no time on tending her bright hair.
In quiet moments of the evening has some hag
    bewitched you with a spell or withered herbs?
A spell removes a neighbour's harvest from the fields;
    a spell halts progress of an angry snake.   20
A spell could draw the moon down from her chariot,
    and would—if not repulsed by clanging cymbals.*
Alas, why whine spells harm a wretched lad?* Or drugs?
    Good looks receive no help from sorcery,
but what *does* hurt is flesh that touched, long kisses granted,
    having pressed together thigh to thigh.
You must remember,* though, not to harass the boy!
    Venus rewards mean acts with punishments.
Don't beg for presents; let a grey-haired lover give
    the presents so soft arms may warm cold limbs.   30
Gold is less cherished than a lad with gleaming smiles
    and no rough stubble that disrupts embraces.
Beneath his shoulders you must place your glowing arms
    and feel contempt for treasures of a king.

at Venus inuenit puero concumbere furtim,
    dum timet et teneros conserit usque sinus,
et dare anhelanti pugnantibus umida linguis
    oscula et in collo figere dente notas.
non lapis hanc gemmaeque iuuant quae frigore sola
    dormiat et nulli sit cupienda uiro.   40
heu sero reuocatur amor seroque iuuentas
    cum uetus infecit cana senecta caput.
tunc studium formae est, coma tunc mutatur ut annos
    dissimulet uiridi cortice tincta nucis;
tollere tunc cura est albos a stirpe capillos
    et faciem dempta pelle referre nouam.
at tu, dum primi floret tibi temporis aetas,
    utere: non tardo labitur illa pede.
neu Marathum torque. puero quae gloria uicto est?
    in ueteres esto dura, puella, senes.   50
parce, precor, tenero. non illi sontica causa est,
    sed nimius luto corpora tingit amor.
uel miser absenti maestas quam saepe querellas
    conicit et lacrimis omnia plena madent.
'quid me spernis?' ait. 'poterat custodia uinci;
    ipse dedit cupidis fallere posse deus.
nota Venus furtiua mihi est, ut lenis agatur
    spiritus, ut nec dent oscula rapta sonum.
et possum media quauis obrepere nocte
    et strepitu nullo clam reserare fores.   60
quid prosunt artes, miserum si spernit amantem
    et fugit ex ipso saeua puella toro,
uel, cum promittit subito sed perfida fallit
    et mihi nox multis est uigilanda malis,
dum mihi uenturam fingo, quodcumque mouetur
    illius credo tunc sonuisse pedes?'
desistas lacrimare, puer. non frangitur illa,
    et tua iam fletu lumina fessa tument.
oderunt, Pholoe, moneo, fastidia diui,
    nec prodest sanctis tura dedisse focis.   70
hic Marathus quondam miseros ludebat amantes,
    nescius ultorem post caput esse deum.

Venus, though, dreams up ways for trysting with a lad—
    while he's afraid and clinging to your chest
and giving sloppy kisses with a feisty tongue
    and making tooth impressions on his neck.
No gems and pearls delight a girl who sleeps alone
    and cold, and is desired by no man.   40
Alas, love is recalled too late, and youth too late,
    when ageing's grey has tinged an older head!
Then there's a quest for beauty, then the hair is changed
    so dye from unripe nutshells* fools the years,
the task then is to pluck white hairs out of their roots
    and, slack skin sloughed off, bring back a new look.*
But use your time of youth while it is first in bloom;
    it does not slip away on sluggish feet!
No torturing Marathus!* Is there glory in
    a beaten boy? Girl, be tough on ancient greybeards!*   50
Please spare the youth! He has no medical defence,*
    but excess passion stains his flesh with yellow.
Indeed, when you're away the wretch just spews his sad
    complaints and drenches everything with tears.
'Why scorn me?'* he declares. 'A guard could have been duped;
    a god himself taught lovers how to cheat.
I know love's secret lore—how breath is softly drawn
    and how a kiss is stolen silently,
and I can sneak around at midnight where I like
    and soundlessly unlock the doors in secret.   60
What good is guile if the vicious girl disdains
    her wretched lover and rejects his bed?
Or when she promises but backs out suddenly,
    and I must wake at night with many troubles.
When I imagine her coming, anything that moves
    then makes me think that I have heard her feet.'
Stop *crying*, lad! She cannot be subdued, and now
    your weary eyes are swelling with your tears!*
I'm warning you, Pholoe, gods despise disdain;
    no incense tossed on sacred altars helps.   70
This same Marathus mocked sad lovers, unaware
    a vengeful god was after his own head.

saepe etiam lacrimas fertur risisse dolentis
  et cupidum ficta detinuisse mora.
nunc omnes odit fastus, nunc displicet illi
  quaecumque opposita est ianua dura sera.
et te poena manet, ni desinis esse superba.
  quam cupies uotis hunc reuocare diem!

It's even said he often laughed at tears of grief
  and held off horny men with fake delays.
Now he detests all pride; *now* he dislikes whatever
  sturdy door that blocks him with a bolt,
and you'll be punished if your vanity persists.
  How you will crave this day's return with prayers!*

9

Quid mihi, si fueras miseros laesurus amores,
  foedera per diuos clam uiolanda dabas?
a miser, et siquis primo periuria celat,
  sera tamen tacitis Poena uenit pedibus.
parcite, caelestes: aequum est impune licere
  numina formosis laedere uestra semel.
lucra petens habili tauros adiungit aratro
  et durum terrae rusticus urget opus.
lucra petituras freta per parentia uentis
  ducunt instabiles sidera certa rates.   10
muneribus meus est captus puer: at deus illa
  in cinerem et liquidas munera uertat aquas.
iam mihi persoluet poenas, puluisque decorem
  detrahet et uentis horrida facta coma.
uretur facies, urentur sole capilli,
  deteret inualidos et uia longa pedes.
admonui quotiens 'auro ne pollue formam:
  saepe solent auro multa subesse mala.
diuitiis captus siquis uiolauit amorem,
  asperaque est illi difficilisque Venus.   20
ure meum potius flamma caput et pete ferro
  corpus et intorto uerbere terga seca.
nec tibi celandi spes sit peccare paranti:
  scit deus occultos qui uetat esse dolos.
ipse deus tacito permisit saepe ministro
  ederet ut multo libera uerba mero.
ipse deus somno domitos emittere uocem
  iussit et inuitos facta tegenda loqui.'
haec ego dicebam: nunc me fleuisse loquentem
  nunc pudet ad teneros procubuisse pedes.   30
tunc mihi iurabas nullo te diuitis auri
  pondere non gemmis uendere uelle fidem,
non tibi si pretium Campania terra daretur,
  non tibi si Bacchi cura Falernus ager.

9

If you were going to abuse my wretched love,
    why make vows by the gods profaned in private?
O wretch, though broken oaths can be concealed at first,
    the punishment still comes on muffled feet.
Show mercy, gods! It's fair to let the gorgeous wrong
    the godheads once without retaliation.
For cash a peasant yokes his bulls to handy ploughs
    and pushes with tough labours through the earth.
Fixed constellations guide the swaying boats that search
    for profit through the waters ruled by wind.*   10
My lad is snared by bribes, but may a god* convert
    that bribery to ash and streaming water!*
Soon he will pay what's due to me, and it will rob
    his looks with dust and wind that tangles hair.
His beauty will be scorched,* his tresses scorched by sun;
    long journeys will erode his pampered feet.*
How often did I warn, 'Don't taint your looks for gold!?
    Often, beneath the gold lurk many evils.
If someone charmed by luxuries dishonours love,
    then Venus is morose and harsh with him.   20
Instead, attack my flesh with steel, and brand my head,
    and slash my shoulders* with a twisted whip!
Nor should you put your hope in hidden plans for sin;
    a god perceives the secret tricks he bans.
A god himself has often let a tactful servant
    speak his mind when there is lots of wine.
A god himself has told those lost in sleep to talk
    and speak of private acts against their will.'
I used to say this: now it shames me that I wept
    while speaking, then collapsed on your soft feet,   30
and then you swore to me you would not sell your trust
    for piles of precious stones or wealth in gold,
not if the price were farmland in Campania,
    not for Falernum's fields* that Bacchus tends.

illis eriperes uerbis mihi sidera caeli
    lucere et pronas fluminis esse uias.
quin etiam flebas, at non ego fallere doctus
    tergebam umentes credulus usque genas.
quid faciam, nisi et ipse fores in amore puellae?
    sic precor exemplo sit leuis illa tuo.   40
o quotiens, uerbis ne quisquam conscius esset
    ipse comes multa lumina nocte tuli!
saepe insperanti uenit tibi munere nostro
    et latuit clausas post adoperta fores.
tunc miser interii, stulte confisus amari;
    nam poteram ad laqueos cautior esse tuos.
quin etiam attonita laudes tibi mente canebam!
    et me nunc nostri Pieridumque pudet.
illa uelim rapida Volcanus carmina flamma
    torreat et liquida deleat amnis aqua.   50
tu procul hinc absis, cui formam uendere cura est
    et pretium plena grande referre manu.
at te, qui puerum donis corrumpere es ausus,
    rideat assiduis uxor inulta dolis
et, cum furtiuo iuuenem lassauerit usu,
    tecum interposita languida ueste cubet.
semper sint externa tuo uestigia lecto
    et pateat cupidis semper aperta domus.
nec lasciua soror dicatur plura bibisse
    pocula uel plures emeruisse uiros.   60
illam saepe ferunt conuiuia ducere Baccho
    dum rota Luciferi prouocet orta diem.
illa nulla queat melius consumere noctem
    aut operum uarias disposuisse uices.
at tua perdidicit, nec tu, stultissime, sentis
    cum tibi non solita corpus ab arte mouet.
tune putas illam pro te disponere crines
    et tenues denso pectere dente comas?
istane persuadet facies auroque lacertos
    uinciat et Tyrio prodeat apta sinu?   70
non tibi sed iuueni cuidam uult bella uideri,
    deuoueat pro quo remque domumque tuam.

Your words could have dissuaded me that starlight shines
 in sky and rivers run on downhill routes!
Indeed, you even wept, though I, unskilled in fraud,
 was still naively wiping tears you shed!
What can I do if you yourself would love a girl?
 I pray that she be fickle just like you!   40
O, so no words were heard, how often have I been
 the steadfast friend who held the lamp at night?*
When hope was gone, she, as my gift, would often come
 to you while veiled and hide behind closed doors.*
Unwisely trusting I was loved, I died back then;
 I should have been more wary of your traps.
However, stunned, I even wrote you tribute poems,
 though now I've shamed the Muses and myself.
May Vulcan* torch that poetry with bursts of flame
 and raging river torrents wash it clean!   50
Just get lost, you who only want to sell your looks
 and come back laden with the loot in hand!
But as for *you*,* who dared corrupt the lad with bribes,
 may your wife's brazen tricks keep mocking you!
And when she's worn out some young lover with a tryst,
 may she lie—listless, fully clothed—with you!
May hints of strangers always linger on your bed
 and may your house stay open for the lustful!
And let it not be said your frisky sister* drains
 more drinking cups or serves more men!   60
They claim she often stretches drinking games until
 the wheels of Lucifer announce the dawn.
No one could better use the night or better set
 positions for her artistry than she,
but your wife learned it all—but you, fool, do not see
 her body move for you with newfound skill.
You don't believe she styles her hair and grooms those precious
 tresses with a fine-toothed comb *for you*?
Is it *your* face that makes her wrap her arms in gold
 and show up decked out in a robe from Tyre?*   70
It's not for you, but some young stud she wants to dazzle
 and for whom she'd give *your* house and assets—

nec facit hoc uitio, sed corpora foeda podagra
   et senis amplexus culta puella fugit.
huic tamen accubuit noster puer! hunc ego credam
   cum trucibus Venerem iungere posse feris.
blanditiasne meas aliis tu uendere es ausus,
   tune aliis demens oscula ferre mea?
tunc flebis cum me uinctum puer alter habebit
   et geret in regno regna superba tuo.   80
at tua tunc me poena iuuet, Venerique merenti
   fixa notet casus aurea palma meos:
HANC TIBI FALLACI RESOLVTVS AMORE TIBVLLVS
   DEDICAT ET GRATA SIS DEA MENTE ROGAT.

not that I blame her, but this girl of fashion flees
  vile, gouty flesh and elderly embraces.
And yet my lad has slept with *him*! I might believe
  that he could couple with an untamed beast!
How dare you sell *my* fondling to other men?
  Weren't you insane to offer them *my* kisses?
Someday you'll cry when some new boy has captured me
  and proudly reigns as king of your domain,   80
then I'll enjoy your torment, and describe my fortunes
  on a golden palm* for worthy Venus:
TIBULLUS, FREED FROM UNTRUE PASSION, OFFERS YOU
  THIS, GODDESS, AND REQUESTS YOUR GRATITUDE.*

10

Quis fuit horrendos primus qui protulit enses?
    quam ferus et uere ferreus ille fuit!
tunc caedes hominum generi tunc proelia nata,
    tunc breuior dirae mortis aperta uia est.
an nihil ille miser meruit, nos ad mala nostra
    uertimus in saeuas quod dedit ille feras?
diuitis hoc uitium est auri, nec bella fuerunt
    faginus astabat cum scyphus ante dapes.
non arces non uallus erat, somnumque petebat
    securus uarias dux gregis inter oues.   10
tunc mihi uita foret uulgi, nec tristia nossem
    arma, nec audissem corde micante tubam.
nunc ad bella trahor, et iam quis forsitan hostis
    haesura in nostro tela gerit latere.
sed patrii seruate Lares: aluistis et idem
    cursarem uestros cum tener ante pedes.
neu pudeat prisco uos esse e stipite factos:
    sic ueteris sedes incoluistis aui.
tunc melius tenuere fidem cum paupere cultu
    stabat in exigua ligneus aede deus.   20
hic placatus erat, seu quis libauerat uuam,
    seu dederat sanctae spicea serta comae;
atque aliquis uoti compos liba ipse ferebat
    postque comes purum filia parua fauum.
at nobis aerata, Lares, depellite tela
    . . .
    . . .
    hostiaque e plena rustica porcus hara.
hanc pura cum veste sequar, myrtoque canistra
    uincta geram, myrto vinctus et ipse caput.   30
sic placeam uobis. alius sit fortis in armis,
    sternat et aduersos Marte fauente duces,
ut mihi potanti possit sua dicere facta
    miles et in mensa pingere castra mero.

10

Who was the first to make horrific two–edged swords?
  How ired and truly iron* that man was!
First murder of the human race, then war was born,
  then quicker ways to grisly death were opened.*
Or was the wretch not guilty? Don't we turn against
  ourselves the evils he designed for beasts?
Gold riches are to blame; there was no warfare when
  a beechwood goblet stood at sacred feasts.*
There were no forts, no palisades, and, safe among
  the mottled ewes,* a shepherd sought his sleep.   10
If I had lived then with those folk, I would not know
  sad wars* or hear a trumpet* with heart pounding.
I'm dragged to war now,* and perhaps some foe already
  bears the weapon that will pierce my side.
But save me, Lares* of my fathers, as you did
  when as a child I scampered at your feet,
and feel no shame that you are made of ancient wood;
  in my ancestral home that's how you lived.
We held a stronger faith back when a wooden god*
  stood poorly decked out in a paltry shrine.   20
He was appeased if someone offered grapes or placed
  a spiky wreath upon a sacred head,*
and he whose prayers were answered brought cake, followed by
  his little daughter with pure honeycomb.
But Lares, turn bronze javelins away from me,*
  [and as I brace to leave for distant lands,
I offer you first fruits from my ancestral fields,]*
  from a full sty, a pig, a farmer's gift.
I'll follow in clean clothes* and bear the basket bound
  with myrtle leaves* with myrtle on my head.   30
I'll please you all this way; let someone else well armed
  and helped by Mars lay hostile leaders low
so as a soldier he can tell me deeds while drinking
  and paint the camp with wine upon the table!*

quis furor est atram bellis arcessere Mortem!
    imminet et tacito clam uenit illa pede.
non seges est infra non uinea culta sed audax
    Cerberus et Stygiae nauita turpis aquae.
illic percussisque genis ustoque capillo
    errat ad obscuros pallida turba lacus.   40
quin potius laudandus hic est quem prole parata
    occupat in parua pigra senecta casa.
ipse suas sectatur oues at filius agnos
    et calidam fesso conparat uxor aquam.
sic ego sim, liceatque caput candescere canis
    temporis et prisci facta referre senem.
interea Pax arua colat. Pax candida primum
    duxit araturos sub iuga curua boues.
Pax aluit uites et sucos condidit uuae,
    funderet ut nato testa paterna merum.   50
Pace bidens uomerque nitent, at tristia duri
    militis in tenebris occupat arma situs.
rusticus e lucoque uehit male sobrius ipse
    uxorem plaustro progeniemque domum.
sed Veneris tunc bella calent, scissosque capillos
    femina perfractas conqueriturque fores.
flet teneras subtusa genas, sed uictor et ipse
    flet sibi dementes tam ualuisse manus.
at lasciuus Amor rixae mala uerba ministrat,
    inter et iratum lentus utrumque sedet.   60
a lapis est ferrumque, suam quicumque puellam
    uerberat: e caelo deripit ille deos.
sit satis e membris tenuem rescindere uestem,
    sit satis ornatus dissoluisse comae,
sit lacrimas mouisse satis. quater ille beatus
    quo tenera irato flere puella potest.
sed manibus qui saeuus erit, scutumque sudemque
    is gerat et miti sit procul a Venere.
at nobis, Pax alma, ueni spicamque teneto,
    perfluat et pomis candidus ante sinus.   70

What is the madness summoning grim Death with wars?
    She's near, and comes unseen on silent feet.
There are no cornfields, no neat vines below, just nasty
    Cerberus* and Styx's filthy oarsman,*
and there, by the murky pools, an ashen mob
    with shredded cheeks and smoking hair* is roaming.   40
Shouldn't we praise instead this man with children sired,
    whom creeping age besieges in his hut?
He trails his sheep, as his son does with lambs, and for
    his weary limbs his wife prepares hot water.
So may I be, and left a head of shining hair
    and an old man's accounts of ancient tales.
Meanwhile, may Peace be tilling fields! Pure Peace first led
    the oxen to the plough beneath curved yokes.
Peace nourished vines and stored grape juice to ensure
    the father's jug could pour wine for his son.   50
With Peace the hoe and ploughshare glitter, while in gloom
    rust fills the hardened soldiers' mournful weapons.*
A farmer, barely sober,* takes his wife and children
    from the grove* by wagon to their house,
but then the wars of Venus* flare up, and the woman
    moans about torn hair and smashed-in doors.
She weeps with bruised and tender cheeks, and yet the victor
    weeps because his foolish hands grew strong,
though playful Love provides some taunting for the brawl
    and calmly sits between the angry couple.*   60
Ah, he is stone and iron who would beat his girl!
    That person tears the gods down from the sky!
It is enough to strip thin clothing off her limbs,
    enough to muss her smartly stylish hair,
enough to stir tears. Joy's quadrupled for the man
    whose rage can make a tender girlfriend weep,
but he whose hands are cruel should take his pike and shield,
    and keep his distance from indulgent Venus.
So come to us while holding cornstalks, fertile Peace,
    and may fruit spring from your resplendent breast!*   70

ELEGIES

Book 2

LIBER SECUNDUS

1

Quisquis adest, faueat: fruges lustramus et agros,
    ritus ut a prisco traditus extat auo.
Bacche, ueni dulcisque tuis e cornibus uua
    pendeat, et spicis tempora cinge, Ceres.
luce sacra requiescat humus, requiescat arator,
    et graue suspenso uomere cesset opus.
soluite uincla iugis: nunc ad praesepia debent
    plena coronato stare boues capite.
omnia sint operata deo: non audeat ulla
    lanificam pensis imposuisse manum.   10
uos quoque abesse procul iubeo: discedat ab aris
    cui tulit hesterna gaudia nocte Venus.
casta placent superis: pura cum ueste uenite
    et manibus puris sumite fontis aquam.
cernite fulgentes ut eat sacer agnus ad aras
    uinctaque post olea candida turba comas.
di patrii, purgamus agros, purgamus agrestes:
    uos mala de nostris pellite limitibus.
neu seges eludat messem fallacibus herbis,
    neu timeat celeres tardior agna lupos.   20
tunc nitidus plenis confisus rusticus agris
    ingeret ardenti grandia ligna foco,
turbaque uernarum, saturi bona signa coloni,
    ludet et ex uirgis exstruet ante casas.
euentura precor. viden ut felicibus extis
    significet placidos nuntia fibra deos?
nunc mihi fumosos ueteris proferte Falernos
    consulis et Chio soluite uincla cado.
uina diem celebrent: non festa luce madere
    est rubor, errantes et male ferre pedes.   30
sed 'bene Messallam' sua quisque ad pocula dicat,
    nomen et absentis singula uerba sonent.

BOOK TWO

1

Be quiet, everyone!* We're cleansing crops and fields,
    a rite still done as forebears passed it on.
Come, Bacchus, and from your horns let sweet grapes hang
    and, Ceres,* wreath your brow with stalks of corn.
Let farmland rest in sacred light;* let farmhands rest.
    Hang up the plough and stop the heavy work.
Take straps from yokes; the oxen in full mangers ought
    to stand now and their heads be crowned with garlands.
Let everything be for the gods;* let no one dare
    suggest a spinner touch her piles of wool.   10
I also ask that all of *you* depart; let those
    whom Venus thrilled last night avoid the altar.
The gods are pleased by abstinence.* Come in pure clothes
    and take water from the spring with your clean hands.
See how the sacred lamb approaches the bright altar,
    then, wreathed in olive leaves, the groups in white.
Gods of our fathers, farms are cleansed, the farmhand cleansed.
    You gods, drive evils from our boundaries!
May cornfields not elude the harvest with sly stalks*
    nor slower lambs be fearful of swift wolves,   20
so then the cheerful peasant, trusting his full fields,
    will pile large logs onto the glowing hearth,
and near it trusted little slaves in groups, the proof
    of rustic wealth, will build stick huts and play.*
My prayers should be fulfilled—see how auspicious signs
    from organ entrails show the gods are calm.
Now bring me smoked Falernian from days of ancient
    consuls and unseal a Chian* jug!
Let's mark the day with wine! It is no shame to soak
    it up at feasts and walk unsteadily,   30
but those with cups should cry out, 'To Messalla's health!'
    and each word sound the absent person's name!*

gentis Aquitanae celeber Messalla triumphis
　et magna intonsis gloria uictor auis,
huc ades aspiraque mihi dum carmine nostro
　redditur agricolis gratia caelitibus.
rura cano rurisque deos: his uita magistris
　desueuit querna pellere glande famem;
illi compositis primum docuere tigillis
　exiguam uiridi fronde operire domum;　　　　　　　　　40
illi etiam tauros primi docuisse feruntur
　seruitium et plaustro supposuisse rotam.
tunc uictus abiere feri, tunc consita pomus,
　tunc bibit irriguas fertilis hortus aquas,
aurea tunc pressos pedibus dedit uua liquores
　mixtaque securo est sobria lympha mero.
rura ferunt messes, calidi cum sideris aestu
　deponit flauas annua terra comas;
rure leuis uerno flores apis ingerit alueo,
　compleat ut dulci sedula melle fauos.　　　　　　　　50
agricola assiduo primum satiatus aratro
　cantauit certo rustica uerba pede,
et satur arenti primum est modulatus auena
　carmen, ut ornatos diceret ante deos;
agricola et minio suffusus, Bacche, rubenti
　primus inexperta duxit ab arte choros;
huic datus a pleno memorabile munus ouili
　dux pecoris paruas auxerat hircus opes.
rure puer uerno primum de flore coronam
　fecit et antiquis imposuit Laribus;　　　　　　　　　60
rure etiam teneris curam exhibitura puellis
　molle gerit tergo lucida uellus ouis;
hinc et femineus labor est, hinc pensa colusque,
　fusus et apposito pollice uersat opus,
atque aliqua assidue textrix operata Mineruae
　cantat et a pulso tela sonat latere.
ipse quoque inter agros interque armenta Cupido
　natus et indomitas dicitur inter equas.
illic indocto primum se exercuit arcu:
　ei mihi, quam doctas nunc habet ille manus!　　　　　70

Messalla, praised for conquering the Aquitaines,*
   the victor, pride of bearded ancestors,
approach and help me, while once more in poetry
   my thanks are given to the farmers' gods.
I praise the farm* and gods of farms; with them as guides,
   life meant not fending hunger off with acorns.
They first taught men to join the rafters and enclose
   a humble dwelling with some leafy boughs.   40
They say too they first taught that bulls were made for work
   and placed a wheel beneath a vehicle,
then savage foods were lost, then seeds for fruit-trees sown,
   then fertile gardens drank from channelled streams,
then golden grapes released their juice to stomping feet
   and sober water mixed with carefree wine.
The country yields the harvest when the scorching star
   of heaven* strips the earth of golden tresses.
In spring swift country bees are busy bearing flowers
   to the hive to fill combs with sweet honey.   50
A farmer, weary of incessant ploughing, first
   recited rustic phrases metrically,*
and once he ate,* it's said, he was the first to sing
   in measures on dry pipes for decked-out gods.
Bacchus, a farmer daubed himself with cinnabar*
   and first inexpertly performed some dances.
He was awarded a most worthy prize—the goat* who led
   all of the flock; it padded his lean assets.
A country boy in spring first made a crown of flowers
   and bestowed it on the ancient Lares,*   60
yet in the country too, the gleaming backs of sheep
   produce soft fleece, a worry for young girls.
From there it's women's work, from there the stint* and distaff.
   A thumb combined with spindle twists the product,
and some weaver, slaving for Minerva, sings,
   and, as weights bang,* the loom is clattering.
Cupid himself, it's said, was also born among
   the flocks and fields, and with unbroken mares.
There he first trained himself to use his untried bow
   and *OH MY** what skilled hands that one now has!   70

nec pecudes uelut ante petit: fixisse puellas
  gestit et audaces perdomuisse uiros.
hic iuueni detraxit opes, hic dicere iussit
  limen ad iratae uerba pudenda senem;
hoc duce custodes furtim transgressa iacentes
  ad iuuenem tenebris sola puella uenit,
et pedibus praetemptat iter, suspensa timore,
  explorat caecas cui manus ante uias.
a miseri quos hic grauiter deus urget, at ille
  felix cui placidus leniter afflat Amor.   80
sancte, ueni dapibus festis, sed pone sagittas
  et procul ardentes hinc, precor, abde faces.
uos celebrem cantate deum pecorique uocate:
  uoce palam pecori, clam sibi quisque uocet,
aut etiam sibi quisque palam, nam turba iocosa
  obstrepit et Phrygio tibia curua sono.
ludite: iam Nox iungit equos, currumque sequuntur
  matris lasciuo sidera fulua choro,
postque uenit tacitus furuis circumdatus alis
  somnus et incerto Somnia nigra pede.   90

Nor does he chase beasts like before—he's thrilled to hurt
   the girls and subjugate courageous men.
He robs this youth; he orders that old man to use
   bad language at an angry woman's door.
With him as guide, a solitary girl in shadows
   slips by napping sentries to her lad,*
and, hanging in suspense, she checks the way each step
   and tests the gloomy paths with outstretched hands.
Ah, people pressured by this god are sad indeed,
   but those Love gently breathes upon are joyous!   80
Holiness, join the sacred feast, but please lay down
   your arrows and withhold your burning torches.
Sing for this honoured god and call him for the herds;
   for cattle call him loudly, softly for yourselves—*
or everyone should bellow, for the merry mob
   and Phrygian curved flute are clamouring!
Play! Night yokes horses now; a lusty choir of golden
   stars pursues its mother's chariot,
and following in silence, wrapped in gloomy wings,
   comes Sleep and murky Dreams on spectral feet.*   90

2

Dicamus bona verba: uenit Natalis ad aras:
  quisquis ades, lingua uir mulierque faue.
urantur pia tura focis, urantur odores,
  quos tener e terra diuite mittit Arabs.
ipse suos Genius adsit uisurus honores,
  cui decorent sanctas mollia serta comas.
illius puro destillent tempora nardo,
  atque satur libo sit madeatque mero.
adnuat et, Cornute, tibi, quodcumque rogabis.
  en age, quid cessas? adnuit ille: roga.   10
auguror, uxoris fidos optabis amores:
  iam reor hoc ipsos edidicisse deos.
nec tibi malueris totum quaecumque per orbem
  fortis arat ualido rusticus arua boue,
nec tibi gemmarum quicquid felicibus Indis
  nascitur, Eoi qua maris unda rubet.
uota cadunt. utinam strepitantibus aduolet alis
  flauaque coniugio uincula portet Amor.
uincula quae maneant semper, dum tarda senectus
  inducat rugas inficiatque comas.   20
hic ueniat, Natalis, auis prolemque ministret,
  ludat et ante tuos turba nouella pedes.

2

Let's speak with joyous words; Birth-Spirit* nears the altar.
  Those present, male or female, hold your tongue!
Let hearths burn holy incense; let them burn perfumes
  some gentle Arab sends from fruitful lands.
The Genius* himself should come to see his rites
  where tender garlands deck his sacred hair.
His temples should be dripping with pure spikenard oil;
  he should be cramming cakes and swilling wine.
He should be nodding yes to what you ask, Cornutus.
  Look! Move! Go ask him! Why delay? . . . HE NODDED! 10
I'm betting you will be praying for a wife's true love;*
  I guess by now the gods themselves have learned that.
Nor would you wish for any fields throughout the world
  that some stout farmer ploughs with his strong ox,
nor gems begotten in abundant India
  where water of the Eastern Sea turns red.
Prayers tumble out.* O may Love soar on beating wings*
  to here and carry wedlock's golden bonds,*
the bonds that last forever as creeping age
  is bringing wrinkles and is tingeing hair.   20
Birth-Spirit, let him come and give grandparents heirs
  so mobs of children frolic at your feet.*

3

Rura meam, Cornute, tenent uillaeque puellam:
    ferreus est eheu quisquis in urbe manet.
ipsa Venus latos iam nunc migrauit in agros,
    uerbaque aratoris rustica discit Amor.
o ego cum aspicerem dominam, quam fortiter illic
    uersarem ualido pingue bidente solum,
agricolaeque modo curuum sectarer aratrum,
    dum subigunt steriles arua serenda boues!
nec quererer quod sol graciles exureret artus,
    laederet et teneras pussula rupta manus.   10
pauit et Admeti tauros formosus Apollo,
    nec cithara intonsae profueruntue comae.
nec potuit curas sanare salubribus herbis:
    quicquid erat medicae uicerat artis amor.
ipse deus solitus stabulis expellere uaccas
    . . .
et miscere nouo docuisse coagula lacte,
    lacteus et mixtis obriguisse liquor.
tunc fiscella leui detexta est uimine iunci,
    raraque per nexus est uia facta sero.   20
o quotiens illo uitulum gestante per agros
    dicitur occurrens erubuisse soror!
o quotiens ausae, caneret dum ualle sub alta,
    rumpere mugitu carmina docta boues!
saepe duces trepidis petiere oracula rebus,
    uenit et a templis irrita turba domum.
saepe horrere sacros doluit Latona capillos
    quos admirata est ipsa nouerca prius.
quisquis inornatumque caput crinesque solutos
    aspiceret, Phoebi quaereret ille comam.   30
Delos ubi nunc, Phoebe, tua est? ubi Delphica Pytho?
    nempe Amor in parua te iubet esse casa.
felices olim, Veneri cum fertur aperte
    seruire aeternos non puduisse deos!

3

Cornutus,* farms and villas occupy my girl.
    Alas, he who can stay in town is iron!
Venus herself has moved on now to open fields
    and Love is learning rustic slang of farmers.
If I could see my mistress, O how hard I'd use
    my trusty hoe to turn the fertile soil
and, as the farmers do, I'd trail a curving plough
    while gelded cattle plough the fields for planting—
and I'd not whine that sunlight burns my slender limbs*
    and broken blisters* hurt my tender hands.   10
Handsome Apollo fed the cattle of Admetus*
    and yet neither lyre nor tresses helped,
nor could he cure his woes with therapeutic plants
    (Love overcame his skill at medicine).*
The god himself was used to driving cows from stalls—
    [it's said he learned their secrets as he worked—]*
and taught techniques of mixing rennet with new milk,
    and the mixed milky liquid turned to solid.
Then they wove a basket tied up with a switch
    and left room in a gap for making whey.*   20
O he would often carry a male calf through fields!
    It's said his sister blushed* when they would meet.
O cows would often butt into his fancy verse
    with mooing as he spoke in high-cliffed valleys!
In crisis leaders often sought his oracles;
    the groups would go home baffled from the shrines.*
Latona* often mourned his unkempt sacred hair,
    which even his stepmother* had admired.
One seeing his limp hair and unembellished head
    would ask if this could be the hair of Phoebus.*   30
Where, Phoebus, is your Delos now? Where's Delphic Pytho?*
    Love, no doubt, assigns you to a hut.
It's said men once were glad when no eternal gods
    felt shame in serving Venus openly.

fabula nunc ille est, sed cui sua cura puella est
　　fabula sit mauolt quam sine amore deus.
at tu, quisquis is est, cui tristi fronte Cupido
　　imperat ut nostra sint tua castra domo

. . .

　　. . .　　　　　　　　　　　　　　　　　　　　　40

ferrea non Venerem sed praedam saecula laudant;
　　praeda tamen multis est operata malis.
praeda feras acies cinxit discordibus armis:
　　hinc cruor hinc caedes mors propiorque uenit.
praeda uago iussit geminare pericula ponto,
　　bellica cum dubiis rostra dedit ratibus.
praedator cupit inmensos obsidere campos
　　ut multa innumera iugera pascat oue;
cui lapis externus curae est urbisque tumultu
　　portatur ualidis multa columna iugis,　　　　　50
claudit et indomitum moles mare, lentus ut intra
　　neglegat hibernas piscis adesse minas.
at mihi laeta trahant Samiae conuiuia testae
　　fictaque Cumana lubrica terra rota.
eheu diuitibus uideo gaudere puellas:
　　iam ueniant praedae si Venus optat opes,
ut mea luxuria Nemesis fluat utque per urbem
　　incedat donis conspicienda meis.
illa gerat uestes tenues quas femina Coa
　　texuit auratas disposuitque uias.　　　　　　60
illi sint comites fusci quos India torret
　　Solis et admotis inficit ignis equis.
illi selectos certent praebere colores
　　Africa puniceum purpureumque Tyros.
nota loquor: regnum ipse tenet quem saepe coegit
　　barbara gypsatos ferre catasta pedes.
at tibi, dura Ceres, Nemesim quae abducis ab urbe,
　　persoluat nulla semina terra fide.
et tu, Bacche tener, iucundae consitor uuae,
　　tu quoque deuotos, Bacche, relinque lacus.　　70
haud impune licet formosas tristibus agris
　　abdere: non tanti sunt tua musta, pater.

He is a scandal now, though one who loves his girl
    prefers a scandal* to a loveless god.
But you,* whoever you may be, who frowning Cupid
    has declared must camp out* in our house,
[be mindful of the way that you obtained your love;
    appeals to Venus won't protect your prize.]*   40
Our iron age applauds not love, but loot of war—
    though loot has played a role in many evils.
Loot fortifies the frontlines with fierce arms that clash,
    so gore, so death and carnage, draw more near.
Loot made the restless oceans twice as perilous
    when it supplied the beaks for rocking vessels.*
A looter longs to occupy the boundless plains
    so many acres feed his countless sheep.
He longs for foreign marble, and his column's hauled
    through city street-life by uncounted oxen.   50
He hems in open seas with walls* so sluggish fish
    can disregard the hazards of the winter,
but, as for me, may jugs from Samos and clay cups
    from Cumae's wheels* prolong the joyous party!
Alas, I see that girls are thrilled by riches now.
    Now let loot come—if Venus chooses wealth—
so that my Nemesis* may drip with luxury
    and glide through town displaying all my gifts!
Let her wear scanty garments women made in Cos
    and artfully arrayed with bands of gold!*   60
Let her have swarthy servants scorched in India
    and stained by fire as the Sun-lord nears.
Let red of Africa* and indigo of Tyre*
    compete to offer her their finest dyes.
I speak what's known; that man—her 'king'—was often forced
    to drag chalked feet upon a foreign scaffold.*
For you, cruel Ceres, luring Nemesis from Rome,
    may Earth not pay a fair return for seed!
And you, soft Bacchus, planter of delightful vines,
    Bacchus, you too must give up your cursed vats!   70
One cannot hide the beautiful in gloomy fields
    without revenge; new wine's not worth it, Father!

o ualeant fruges, ne sint modo rure puellae.
  glans alat et prisco more bibantur aquae.
glans aluit ueteres, et passim semper amarunt.
  quid nocuit sulcos non habuisse satos?
tunc, quibus aspirabat Amor, praebebat aperte
  mitis in umbrosa gaudia valle Venus.
nullus erat custos, nulla exclusura dolentes
  ianua. si fas est, mos, precor, ille redi.   80

. . .

  horrida uillosa corpora ueste tegant.
nunc, si clausa mea est, si copia rara uidendi,
  heu miserum, laxam quid iuuat esse togam?
ducite. ad imperium dominae sulcabimus agros:
  non ego me uinclis uerberibusque nego.

O let fruit vanish so no girls are in the country!
    Let's eat old-fashioned nuts and drink just water!
Nuts fed the ancients*—and they always loved impulsively!
    What was the harm not having seeds in furrows?
Back then for those Love breathed on, gentle Venus brought
    them public pleasures in the shaded valleys.
There were no guards, no sad displays outside a door.*
    If possible, please bring this practice back!   80
[May Love restore for us this joyous way of life;]*
    may quaking limbs be cloaked in clothes of fur!*
If now she's kept from me, if gazes are a fluke,
    alas, poor wretch, what good's a flowing toga?*
Lead me off! I will plough fields as my mistress orders.
    I will never shrink from chains and lashes!*

4

Sic mihi seruitium uideo dominamque paratam:
    iam mihi, libertas illa paterna, uale.
seruitium sed triste datur, teneorque catenis,
    et numquam misero uincla remittit Amor,
et seu quid merui seu nil peccauimus, urit.
    uror: io, remoue, saeua puella, faces.
o ego ne possim tales sentire dolores,
    quam mallem in gelidis montibus esse lapis,
stare uel insanis cautes obnoxia uentis
    naufraga quam uasti tunderet unda maris!   10
nunc et amara dies et noctis amarior umbra est:
    omnia nunc tristi tempora felle madent.
nec prosunt elegi nec carminis auctor Apollo:
    illa caua pretium flagitat usque manu.
ite procul, Musae, si non prodestis amanti:
    non ego uos ut sint bella canenda colo,
nec refero solisque uias et qualis, ubi orbem
    compleuit, uersis luna recurrit equis.
ad dominam faciles aditus per carmina quaero:
    ite procul, Musae, si nihil ista ualent.   20
at mihi per caedem et facinus sunt dona paranda,
    ne iaceam clausam flebilis ante domum,
aut rapiam suspensa sacris insignia fanis:
    sed Venus ante alios est uiolanda mihi:
illa malum facinus suadet dominamque rapacem
    dat mihi: sacrilegas sentiat illa manus.
o pereat quicumque legit uiridesque smaragdos
    et niueam Tyrio murice tingit ouem!
hic dat auaritiae causas et Coa puellis
    uestis et e Rubro lucida concha mari.   30
haec fecere malas, hinc clauim ianua sensit,
    et coepit custos liminis esse canis.
sed pretium si grande feras, custodia uicta est
    nec prohibent claues et canis ipse tacet.

4

I see that I have gained both bondage and a mistress.*
    Farewell to native freedoms now for me!
Still, sadly, service is imposed and I'm in chains,
    and for a wretch Love never loosens bonds,*
and whether I have earned it or not sinned, it burns.
    I burn. *Ouch!* Heartless girl, remove the torch!*
O how I wish I'd never feel these kinds of pains!
    I'd rather be a stone on some cold peak
or stand a cliff exposed to wildness of the winds*
    which ship-destroying waves of vast sea pummel.   10
The day is bitter now, and gloom of night more bitter;
    now each moment drips with sullen gall.
Apollo, source of verse, and elegy are worthless;
    her cupped hand keeps begging some reward.
Muses, be gone if you can't offer lovers help!
    I'm not pursuing you to sing of wars,*
or rehash solar routes or how the moon turns horses
    and returns once she has come full circle.*
Through verse I ask for easy access to my mistress.*
    Muses, be gone if that cannot succeed.   20
However, I must get her gifts by theft or gore
    so I don't weep outside her closed-up house
or grab the sacred emblems hanging in the shrines—
    but first in line to be profaned is Venus.
She counsels crime, and leaves me with a grasping girl.
    May she experience unholy hands!*
O let whoever deals green emeralds and stains
    the snowy fleece with dye from Tyre* be damned!
Along with brilliant Red Sea pearls and Coan fashion,*
    they are causes of the greed in girls!   30
It makes them wicked, so an entrance feels a key*
    and on the steps a dog begins its watch,
but if you carry lots of cash, the guard is dodged,
    no keys exclude, and that same dog is silent.

heu quicumque dedit formam caelestis auarae,
    quale bonum multis attulit ille malis!
hinc fletus rixaeque sonant, haec denique causa
    fecit ut infamis nunc deus esset Amor.
at tibi quae pretio uictos excludis amantes
    eripiant partas uentus et ignis opes.   40
quin tua tunc iuuenes spectent incendia laeti
    nec quisquam flammae sedulus addat aquam.
heu ueniet tibi mors, nec erit qui lugeat ullus
    nec qui det maestas munus in exsequias.
at bona quae nec auara fuit, centum licet annos
    uixerit, ardentem flebitur ante rogum;
atque aliquis senior ueteres ueneratus amores
    annua constructo serta dabit tumulo,
et 'bene' discedens dicet 'placideque quiescas,
    terraque securae sit super ossa leuis.'   50
uera quidem moneo, sed prosunt quid mihi uera?
    illius est nobis lege colendus Amor.
quin etiam sedes iubeat si uendere auitas,
    ite sub imperium sub titulumque, Lares.
quidquid habet Circe quidquid Medea ueneni,
    quidquid et herbarum Thessala terra gerit
et quod, ubi indomitis gregibus Venus afflat amores,
    hippomanes cupidae stillat ab inguine equae,
si modo me placido uideat Nemesis mea uultu,
    mille alias herbas misceat illa, bibam.   60

Whichever god gave beauty to a greedy girl,
  alas, he brought much evil with the good,
and so the sobs and brawls resound; in short, it's why
  Love is a god who's disrespected now,
but as for you, who shut out lovers short on cash,
  may wind and fire* savage what you gain!   40
Indeed, may happy lads then watch your assets burn
  —and nobody be zealous dousing flames!
Alas, when death arrives for you, no one will mourn
  or offer tributes at your sad last rites!
Although a hundred years old, she who's kind and selfless
  will be mourned beside the burning pyre,
and some old fellow honouring lost love shall place
  his garlands on the mounded grave each year
and say while leaving, 'May you rest in peace and well,
  and earth be light upon your tranquil ashes.'*   50
My warning's true, although what good is truth to me?
  It's by her rules that we must nourish love!
Yes, and if she insists my forebears' house be sold,
  go, Lares, stand beneath the for-sale sign!*
Whatever potions Circe or Medea have,
  whatever Thessaly's soil yields in drugs*
or even piss discharged from groins of mares in heat
  as Venus blows her passions on wild herds,*
if my Nemesis will calmly look at me,
  let her combine a thousand drugs! I'll drink.   60

5

Phoebe, faue: nouus ingreditur tua templa sacerdos:
    huc age cum cithara carminibusque ueni.
nunc te uocales impellere pollice chordas,
    nunc precor ad laudes flectere uerba mea.
ipse triumphali deuinctus tempora lauro
    dum cumulant aras ad tua sacra ueni.
sed nitidus pulcherque ueni: nunc indue uestem
    sepositam, longas nunc bene pecte comas,
qualem te memorant Saturno rege fugato
    uictori laudes concinuisse Ioui.   10
tu procul euentura uides, tibi deditus augur
    scit bene quid fati prouida cantet auis;
tuque regis sortes, per te praesentit haruspex
    lubrica signauit cum deus exta notis;
te duce Romanos numquam frustrata Sibylla,
    abdita quae senis fata canit pedibus.
Phoebe, sacras Messallinum sine tangere chartas
    uatis, et ipse, precor, quid canat illa doce.
haec dedit Aeneae sortes postquam ille parentem
    dicitur et raptos sustinuisse Lares.   20
nec fore credebat Romam cum maestus ab alto
    Ilion ardentes respiceretque deos.
Romulus aeternae nondum formauerat urbis
    moenia, consorti non habitanda Remo,
sed tunc pascebant herbosa Palatia uaccae
    et stabant humiles in Iouis arce casae.
lacte madens illic suberat Pan ilicis umbrae
    et facta agresti lignea falce Pales,
pendebatque uagi pastoris in arbore uotum
    garrula siluestri fistula sacra deo,   30
fistula cui semper decrescit arundinis ordo,
    nam calamus cera iungitur usque minor.
at qua Velabri regio patet, ire solebat
    exiguus pulsa per uada linter aqua.

5

Phoebus, protect the novice entering your shrine;
   come quickly to perform with song and lyre.*
Your thumbs now strum the singing strings; I pray that you
   now change my lyrics into words of praise.
With temples wreathed in hero's laurel while they load
   the altars, come into your sacred shrine,
but enter bright and beautiful, then wear the robe
   that's set aside* and comb your tresses well
as they recall you did when Saturn was dethroned;
   you sang the praises of the victor, Jove.*   10
You see the distant future; your devoted augur
   knows what's fated when a bird is singing,
and you guide the lots; through you a seer divines
   a god's intentions with some slimy entrails.*
With you the lead, the Sibyl sings hexameters*
   of secret fate that have not misled Romans.
Let Messalinus touch the prophet's sacred scrolls,
   Phoebus, and teach him please what she is chanting.
It's said she gave Aeneas lots once he had carried
   off his father and the rescued Lares.*   20
He did not trust Rome's future when, grim on a height,
   he gazed at burning gods of Ilium.
Romulus had not planned the timeless city's* walls
   in which his brother Remus* would not live,
but back then cattle grazed a grassy Palatine*
   and grubby hovels stood upon Jove's hill.*
There, dripping milk, was Pan below a shady oak
   with wooden Pales* a field hook had fashioned,
and on the tree there hung a roving shepherd's gift:
   a breezy reed-pipe offered to the tree-god,*   30
a pipe with reeds that keep on shrinking in a row
   because wax joins each shaft to one that's smaller,
and, where the precinct of Velabrum* now extends,
   a tiny boat would row through shallow shoals.

illa saepe gregis diti placitura magistro
    ad iuuenem festa est uecta puella die,
cum qua fecundi redierunt munera ruris,
    caseus et niueae candidus agnus ovis.
Impiger Aenea, uolitantis frater Amoris,
    Troica qui profugis sacra uehis ratibus,   40
iam tibi Laurentes assignat Iuppiter agros,
    iam uocat errantes hospita terra Lares.
illic sanctus eris, cum te ueneranda Numici
    unda deum caelo miserit indigetem.
ecce super fessas uolitat Victoria puppes:
    tandem ad Troianos diua superba uenit.
ecce mihi lucent Rutulis incendia castris:
    iam tibi praedico, barbare Turne, necem.
ante oculos Laurens castrum murusque Lauini est
    Albaque ab Ascanio condita Longa duce.   50
te quoque iam uideo, Marti placitura sacerdos
    Ilia, Vestales deseruisse focos,
concubitusque tuos furtim vittasque iacentes
    et cupidi ad ripas arma relicta dei.
carpite nunc, tauri, de septem montibus herbas
    dum licet: hic magnae iam locus urbis erit.
Roma, tuum nomen terris fatale regendis
    qua sua de caelo prospicit arua Ceres,
quaque patent ortus et qua fluitantibus undis
    Solis anhelantes abluit amnis equos.   60
Troia quidem tunc se mirabitur et sibi dicet
    uos bene tam longa consuluisse uia.
uera cano: sic usque sacras innoxia laurus
    uescar et aeternum sit mihi uirginitas.'
haec cecinit uates et te sibi, Phoebe, uocauit,
    iactauit fusas et caput ante comas.
quidquid Amalthea, quidquid Marpesia dixit
    Herophile, Phyto Graia quod admonuit,
quasque Aniena sacras Tiburs per flumina sortes
    portarat sicco pertuleratque sinu: 70
haec fore dixerunt belli mala signa cometen,
    multus ut in terras deplueretque lapis,

Often delighting some rich shepherd, it is there
    a girl was brought on feast-day to her lad
who brought back from the overflowing fields these gifts:
    a snowy ewe's white lamb along with cheese.
'Flitting Love's brother,* resolute Aeneas, whose
    nomadic boat transported Trojan relics,   40
Jupiter now assigns to you Laurentum's fields;*
    the friendly farmland now calls the straying Lares.
There you will be divine, a local god of Heaven,*
    when worshipped waves of Numicus transport you.
Look! Victory ascends above the weary ships!
    At last the haughty goddess visits Trojans!
Look! Fires in Rutulian camps glow for me;
    Now, savage Turnus,* I predict your fall!
I scan Lavinium's wall* and Laurentum's fort,
    and King Ascanius' Alba Longa.*   50
I also see you, Ilia,* the priestess Mars
    will favour, as you fled the Vestal hearths—
your furtive tryst, discarded sacred bands, and armour
    of a lustful god left by the river.
Bulls, grab the grasses while you can from Seven Hills!*
    A mighty city's site will be right here!
Your name is destined, Rome, for ruler of the Earth
    where Ceres looks from Heaven on her fields,
and where dawn spreads and where the tides of oceans wash
    the Sun-God's panting steeds with waves of spray.   60
Troy* then will truly marvel at itself and tell
    itself you served her well by your long journey.
I sing the truth, and therefore may I taste unscathed
    the sacred laurel and remain a virgin.'
So Sibyl sang, and called you, Phoebus, down to her,
    and tossed her flowing hair before her face.
Amalthea and the Marpessan Herophile
    agreed, and Greek Phoeto warned of this,
as did the sacred lots that Tibur's Sibyl took
    and carried, breast dry, through the Anio;*   70
they said a comet* would appear, an evil sign
    of battle that would shower land with rocks.*

atque tubas atque arma ferunt strepitantia caelo
    audita, et lucos praecinuisse fugam.
ipsum etiam solem defectum lumine uidit
    iungere pallentes nubilus annus equos,
et simulacra deum lacrimas fudisse tepentes,
    fataque uocales praemonuisse boues.
haec fuerunt olim, sed tu iam mitis, Apollo,
    prodigia indomitis merge sub aequoribus,   80
et succensa sacris crepitet bene laurea flammis
    omine quo felix et satur annus erit.
laurus ubi bona signa dedit, gaudete, coloni:
    distendet spicis horrea plena Ceres,
oblitus et musto feriet pede rusticus uuas
    dolia dum magni deficiantque lacus,
ac madidus Baccho sua festa Palilia pastor
    concinet: a stabulis tunc procul este, lupi.
ille leuis stipulae solemnes potus aceruos
    accendet flammas transilietque sacras,   90
et fetus matrona dabit natusque parenti
    oscula comprensis auribus eripiet,
nec taedebit auum paruo aduigilare nepoti
    balbaque cum puero dicere uerba senem.
tunc operata deo pubes discumbet in herba,
    arboris antiquae qua leuis umbra cadit,
aut e ueste sua tendent umbracula sertis
    uincta, coronatus stabit et ipse calix.
at sibi quisque dapes et festas exstruet alte
    caespitibus mensas caespitibusque torum.   100
ingeret hic potus iuuenis maledicta puellae
    postmodo quae uotis irrita facta uelit;
nam ferus ille suae plorabit sobrius idem
    et se iurabit mente fuisse mala.
pace tua pereant arcus pereantque sagittae,
    Phoebe, modo in terris erret inermis Amor.
ars bona sed postquam sumpsit sibi tela Cupido
    eheu quam multis ars dedit ista malum,
et mihi praecipue iaceo qui saucius annum
    et faueo morbo cum iuuat ipse dolor.   110

Men say they heard resounding arms and horns above,
    and that the sacred grove foretold a rout.
That shrouded year* would even see the Sun himself,
    still fading, harness shrouded ghostly steeds,
and images of gods were shedding tepid tears,
    and talking cattle prophesied disasters.
This came to pass, but now, Apollo, be indulgent;
    submerge these prodigies beneath wild seas.   80
How well the kindled laurel snaps in sacred flames,
    a sign the year will be both rich and lucky!
When laurel gives propitious news, rejoice, fieldworkers!
    Ceres jams the bulging barns with corn
and then the peasant, smeared with grape-juice, stomps the grapes
    until the tubs and cistern overflow
and, drunk, a shepherd at Palilia,* his feast,
    will sing; steer clear of stables then, you wolves!
He'll light the customary piles of flimsy straw
    while drunk and leap across the sacred flames,   90
and then his wife will have a baby, and the child
    will grab his father's ears to get some kisses;
no grandfather will balk at keeping grandsons safe,
    nor an old man at spouting baby talk.
Then, honouring a god, the throngs will lie on grass
    where shifting shadows fall from ancient trees
or spread their clothing on the bowers trimmed with garlands,
    and put the chalice, wreathed itself, in place,
and all of them will pile their food up at the feast,
    with turf a table and with turf a couch.   100
Here a drunk lad hurls curses at his girlfriend—after
    which he'll wish his deeds undone in prayers
since he will sob while sober for his savagery
    and swear that he had been out of his mind.
With your consent may bows be banned and arrows banned,
    Phoebus, so Love may wander Earth unarmed.
Skill's fine, but after Cupid took up arms himself,
    alas that skill produced such punishment—
and mostly mine—while wounded I have lain a year
    and clung to sickness while my pain was joy.*   110

usque cano Nemesim, sine qua uersus mihi nullus
      uerba potest iustos aut reperire pedes.
at tu, nam diuum seruat tutela poetas,
      praemoneo, uati parce puella sacro,
ut Messallinum celebrem cum praemia belli
      ante suos currus oppida uicta feret.
ipse gerens laurus, lauro deuinctus agresti
      miles 'io' magna uoce 'triumphe' canet.
tunc Messalla meus pia det spectacula turbae
      et plaudat curru praetereunte pater.   120
annue: sic tibi sint intonsi, Phoebe, capilli,
      sic tua perpetuo sit tibi casta soror.

I always sing of Nemesis; I couldn't find
  a proper word or foot of verse without her.
But girl, I'm warning you! Pity a sacred bard
  because gods serve as poets' guardians,
so I may honour Messalinus when, for plunder,
  he drives conquered towns* before his steeds.
Wearing his laurel, wreathed in laurel from the fields,
  his troops would cry, 'O triumph!' with loud voices,
then may my dear Messalla give the crowd a show,
  and cheer the passing chariot as father.   120
Phoebus, agree so that your hair remains unshorn,
  and so your sister is forever chaste!

6

Castra Macer sequitur: tenero quid fiet Amori?
    sit comes et collo fortiter arma gerat?
et seu longa uirum terrae uia seu uaga ducent
    aequora, cum telis ad latus ire uolet?
ure, puer, quaeso, tua qui ferus otia liquit,
    atque iterum erronem sub tua signa uoca.
quod si militibus parces, erit hic quoque miles,
    ipse leuem galea qui sibi portet aquam.
castra peto, ualeatque Venus ualeantque puellae:
    et mihi sunt uires et mihi facta tuba est.   10
magna loquor, sed magnifice mihi magna locuto
    excutiunt clausae fortia uerba fores.
iuraui quotiens rediturum ad limina numquam!
    cum bene iuraui, pes tamen ipse redit.
acer Amor, fractas utinam tua tela sagittas,
    si licet, extinctas aspiciamque faces!
tu miserum torques, tu me mihi dira precari
    cogis et insana mente nefanda loqui.
iam mala finissem leto, sed credula uitam
    Spes fouet et fore cras semper ait melius.   20
Spes alit agricolas, Spes sulcis credit aratis
    semina quae magno faenore reddat ager.
haec laqueo uolucres haec captat harundine pisces
    cum tenues hamos abdidit ante cibus.
Spes etiam ualida solatur compede uinctum:
    crura sonant ferro, sed canit inter opus.
Spes facilem Nemesim spondet mihi, sed negat illa:
    ei mihi, ne uincas, dura puella, deam.
parce, per immatura tuae precor ossa sororis:
    sic bene sub tenera parua quiescat humo.   30
illa mihi sancta est, illius dona sepulcro
    et madefacta meis serta feram lacrimis,
illius ad tumulum fugiam supplexque sedebo
    et mea cum muto fata querar cinere.

6

Macer* is called up. What will come of tender Love?
  Be friends and bravely lug gear on his neck?
And if the land and restless ocean lead the man
  on journeys will he want to join him armed?
I ask, boy,* that you singe the clod who fled your peace
  and call the rebel* back beneath your banner,
but if you spare the troops, I'll soldier on as well
  and carry sips of water in my helmet.
I'm off to camp, and no more girls, and no more Venus,
  and I am strong and destined for the trumpet!   10
I brag, but when I've bragged with braggadocio
  the slamming doors* reject my brazen words.
I swore so often not to go back to her door,
  yet when I swore, my wilful feet returned.
Cruel Love, if only it were possible I'd see
  your darts and arrows smashed and torches* snuffed.
You torture a poor wretch; you make me curse myself
  and utter blasphemies dementedly.
Death would have stopped these wrongs, but trustful Hope
  supports life and still says tomorrow's better.   20
Hope nourishes the farmer; Hope entrusts ploughed rows
  with seed that fields repay with handsome profits.
She traps the birds with snares, the fish with rods of reed
  when bait conceals a slender hook within.
Hope also comforts the strong man controlled by chains;
  leg-irons jangle, but he sings at work.
Hope sells me 'easy' Nemesis*—but she declines!
  Oh my, tough girl, you don't defeat a goddess!
Please, by your sister's doll-like bones* show mercy so
  the child may rest well under the soft earth.   30
For me she's sacred, and upon her tomb I'll place
  some presents and a garland drenched in tears.
I'll fly then to her grave and sit, a suppliant,
  and moan about my fate to silent ash.

non feret usque suum te propter flere clientem:
   illius ut uerbis sis mihi lenta ueto,
ne tibi neglecti mittant mala somnia Manes
   maestaque sopitae stet soror ante torum,
qualis ab excelsa praeceps delapsa fenestra
   uenit ad infernos sanguinolenta lacus.   40
desino, ne dominae luctus renouentur acerbi:
   non ego sum tanti ploret ut illa semel,
nec lacrimis oculos digna est foedare loquaces.
   lena nocet nobis; ipsa puella bona est.
lena uetat miserum Phryne furtimque tabellas
   occulto portans itque reditque sinu.
saepe ego cum dominae dulces a limine duro
   agnosco uoces, haec negat esse domi.
saepe ubi nox mihi promissa est, languere puellam
   nuntiat aut aliquas extimuisse minas.   50
tunc morior curis, tunc mens mihi perdita fingit
   quisue meam teneat quot teneatue modis;
tunc tibi, lena, precor diras: satis anxia uiuas,
   mouerit e uotis pars quotacumque deos.

She will not bear her client's constant tears for you;
    by her command I can't allow your coldness
so your slighted sister won't remain beside
    the bed and send disturbing dreams in sleep
as when she came bloodspattered to the lake below
    by falling headfirst from an upstairs window.*   40
I stop so I won't stir my lady's bitter grief;
    I am not worth a single sob from her.
Nor is it right that tears should mar expressive eyes.
    Her madam's mean;* the girl herself is fine.
Phryne* the bawd excludes this wretch—she comes and goes
    while bringing secret letters in her chest.
At her cruel doorstep, where I often hear her sweet
    expressions, *she* denies she is at home.
The madam often says she's sick or frightened by
    some omens when a night was booked for me,   50
then fretting kills me, and then panic strikes my mind
    about who holds my love (and in which ways);
Madam, I pray you're cursed. You'll live with ample dread
    if something in my prayers affects the gods.

EXPLANATORY NOTES

BOOK ONE

ELEGY I.I

First poems of a collection were programmatic, setting out the author's distinctive approach to the genre and giving the audience an idea of the themes and motifs which are to dominate the book. Here Tib.'s dream-world of a simple rural existence on his modest ancestral farm, inspired by traditional religion and love, is contrasted with the harsh life of the soldier, devoted to the acquisition of wealth and glory.

In the first half of the poem (1–40) soldiering in pursuit of wealth is rejected in favour of a simple rural life spent in pious devotion to the rustic gods. In the second half (53–74) soldiering in pursuit of glory, as exemplified by his patron Messalla, is rejected in Tib.'s case in favour of a life in the service of love. The central section (41–52) links these two halves by summing up the earlier rustic themes and gradually introducing the theme of love for his mistress, Delia, which is to dominate the second half. In a final concluding section (75–8) the main themes of love, war, wealth, and the simple country life are recapitulated.

Unlike his contemporary, the elegist Propertius, whose mistress Cynthia dominates his opening poem, Tib. delays the love theme until much later in the elegy. Delia is not mentioned until line 57. Love is just one of the elements of his ideal existence.

Tib.'s opening elegy, then, exemplifies the type of poetry to follow: a discreet blend of bucolic and emotional themes, inspired both by the Hellenistic Greek and the contemporary Roman poetic tradition, especially the *Eclogues* and *Georgics* of Virgil.

4 *Mars' trumpets*: war trumpets. Loud military horns were used by the commanders in the field to give such signals as the start of battle.

11–12 *lonely tree-stumps ... weathered stone*: boundary markers in the fields, seen as representations of the boundary god Terminus and decorated with garlands on his feast day, 23 February.

14 *the farmer-god*: intentionally vague. Perhaps a reference to the Roman rustic god Silvanus, to whom offerings of first fruits were made at harvest time.

15 *golden Ceres*: a native Italian harvest goddess (hence the epithet 'golden'), equivalent to the Greek Demeter.

17 *red Priapus*: a red-painted fertility god with a huge phallus and a reaping hook (scythe), used as a scarecrow in gardens and orchards. He was not a native Italian god, but arrived from Asia Minor via Greece.

19 *Lares*: guardian spirits of the hearth and farm, often depicted as young men holding a drinking horn and dancing. As promoters of fertility in the fields they were especially important to Tib., who mentions them a number of times in his works.

20 *of threadbare land that once was prosperous*: Tib.'s ancestral estates, like those of Propertius and Horace, may have suffered in the land confiscations of the civil wars that followed the battle of Philippi.

27 *Dog Star's heat*: the Dog Star, Sirius, rose shortly after the summer solstice. Its intense and destructive heat is a commonplace of ancient literature.

36 *sprinkle gentle Pales with some milk*: a native Italian goddess (or, sometimes, god) who presided over the fields and herds. Her festival was on 21 April, Rome's foundation day, and is described in detail by Tib. at 2.5.87–104. Its main purpose was the purification of the fields and shepherds. As a peaceful deity, she was given only non-blood offerings of milk.

47 *Austral winds*: the south wind, Auster, was supposed to bring clouds and rain.

53 *Messalla*: Tib.'s patron, the aristocrat M. Valerius Messalla Corvinus, an important military figure and literary patron (see the Introduction, p. ix). He took a keen interest in his own ancestry and added to his family's long line of victories by his own campaigns, especially in Illyria, Egypt, and Aquitania (celebrated in Elegy 1.7).

54 *spoils of war*: enemy spoils were fastened up before the door or in the hall of the triumphant general's house.

55 *Chains of a gorgeous girl*: the image is of the lover as the chained prisoner or slave of his mistress. It is introduced naturally after the mention of the spoils of war in 54, which suggest chained prisoners.

56 *doorman*: the excluded lover imagines himself as his mistress's slave door-keeper. These were often chained at the house-door.

57 *Delia*: this is the first mention of his mistress's name, by which she is addressed again at 61 and 67.

59 *May I behold you*: as a lover Tib. wants to die facing his mistress, in contrast with the soldier who would die facing the enemy.

67–8 *Do not do damage . . . spare your tender cheeks*: Delia could weep and unbind her hair at Tib.'s funeral, but more extreme tokens of grief such as cutting her hair and scratching her cheeks would spoil her beauty and thus pain his departed spirit.

70 *his features cloaked in gloom*: literally 'his head veiled in darkness', a striking and original image, perhaps influenced by pictures of Death personified in art or on the stage.

75 *a good soldier and good leader*: the image of the soldier of love was common in elegy. Ovid devotes a whole poem to the idea at *Amores* 1.9.

77 *by stacks I stored*: 'stacks' translates the Latin *acervo*, literally 'a heap of produce'. This picks up the use of the same word in line 9 above, where it is translated as 'stacked crops'.

ELEGY 1.2

In this poem Tibullus provides a variation on the song of the shut-out lover, a theme already hinted at in the first elegy (1.1.56) and frequently alluded to elsewhere in his work (e.g. 1.5.67–8, 2.3.77–8, 2.4.19). Known technically as the *paraklausithyron (sc. melos)* or '(Song) at the Locked Door', it is also found in Propertius 1.16, where the door itself is made to speak, and Ovid, *Amores* 1.6, where the song is addressed not to the girl but to the door-keeper.

Delia has been put under guard by her husband (5–6). Tib. is locked outside her door and calls for wine to drown his sorrows (1–4). He appeals to the door to let him in (7–14) and to Delia to come out to him (15–16). He reminds her that Venus helps lovers in general (16–24) and himself in particular (25–42). He has also enlisted the aid of a witch in their affair (43–66). Unlike his rival who left Delia and went off to war in search of wealth, Tib. would prefer a simple life with her in the country (67–80). He promises atonement to Venus if any impiety of his toward her has caused his present suffering (81–8), threatens a mocking bystander (89–98), and ends with an appeal for Venus to spare him (99–100).

1 *Pour more unwatered wine*: as emerges later, Tib. must be addressing a slave outside his mistress's locked door. The ancients normally drank their wine mixed with water and the use of neat wine here is intended to induce sleep. The inspiration for the first four lines of the poem comes from a Greek epigram by Meleager, *Palatine Anthology* 12.49: 'Drink strong wine, unhappy lover, and Bromios (Bacchus), giver of forgetfulness, will send to sleep the flame of your love for the boy. Drink strong wine and, draining the cup full of vine juice, strike out hateful pain from your heart.'

3 *when my brow is Bacchus-bludgeoned*: literally 'when my brow has been bludgeoned by much Bacchus'. The wine god here is used as a metonymy for wine itself.

16 *Venus*: traditionally the protectress of lovers.

18 *with hairpin*: the exact meaning of the Latin *fixo dente* here is disputed. 'Hairpin' reflects the surreptitious action of 'picking the lock'. One explanation is that the 'tooth' (*dente*) refers to a single spike, fixed (*fixo*) to a wooden handle, which Delia could use as a skeleton key to open the door from the inside.

29 *A person gripped by love should travel safe and blessed*: the first extant appearance of the idea of the lover as a sacred person, divinely protected from harm. Tib. perhaps develops the theme from Greek epigram where lovers are depicted as feeling no fear.

36 *thefts*: a technical term in Roman elegy for lovers' intrigues.

42 *the child of savage seas and blood*: Venus (Aphrodite in Greek) sprang from
    the gore and foam produced when Chronos castrated his father Uranus
    and threw his genitals into the sea (Hesiod, *Theogony* 176–206).

43 *an honest witch*: in elegy, as in real life, witchcraft was commonly associ-
    ated with inducing or repelling love (cf. Propertius 1.1.19–22). It is a
    frequent theme in Tib. (cf. 1.5.41–4, 1.8.17–24, 2.4.55).

53 *Medea's toxic herbs*: Medea, the Colchian princess, who by her magic
    enabled Jason to win the golden fleece, was the prime example of a witch
    in antiquity. Books purporting to contain her spells circulated at Rome in
    Tib.'s time.

54 *Hecate*: Greek goddess of the underworld, worshipped by witches, and
    Medea's patron deity. Dogs were supposed to be her constant com-
    panions and were offered to her in sacrifice.

56 *three times*: the number three had magical significance in the ancient
    world.

57 *He*: i.e. the husband.

64 *dark gods*: i.e. the gods of the underworld.

69 *Let him repel Cilicia's defeated troops*: we now gather that Delia's husband
    was fighting abroad in Cilicia, and for this reason had put a guard on
    Delia during his absence. Cilicia, now part of modern Turkey, had been
    visited on campaign by Messalla. The natives were notorious for their
    toughness and piracy. It was a rich province (producing saffron) and a
    good source of booty.

77 *a bed from Tyre*: i.e. a couch covered with Tyrian purple, a luxury
    item. The Phoenician port of Tyre had invented the process of dyeing
    cloth purple from a substance found in a vein of various species of
    shellfish.

80 *water's lilting sounds*: possibly a fountain playing in the inner court,
    although we hear of particularly luxurious dwellings (like Pliny's Tuscan
    villa) having streams diverted to pass through the bedrooms.

84 *snatched some garland*: possibly to pin to Delia's door. Shut-out lovers
    regularly left such offerings.

96 *stop her handmaid in the marketplace*: the theme of the mistress's maid as a
    go-between is common in comedy.

98 *spat on his own tender breast*: spitting, often into the bosom, was a common
    means of warding off evil, and especially, as here, of avoiding contagion
    from a lunatic.

ELEGY 1.3

Tib. has fallen sick on the island of Phaeacia (Corcyra), while accompanying
Messalla on official business to the East. The expedition is probably the one
referred to later at 1.7.13ff., undertaken by Messalla at the request of Octavian
sometime after the battle of Actium (31 BC).

The elegy consists of a series of reflections evoked in the poet by this situation. Tib. bids farewell to Messalla and prays that death will spare him in a foreign land in the absence of Delia and his family (1–10). Reflections on his parting from Delia in Rome (11–22) lead to a prayer to Delia's favourite goddess, Isis, to provide a cure. Delia's worship of Egyptian Isis is contrasted with his own preference for the traditional Roman Penates and Lares (23–34). Saturn's Golden Age, a time of rustic simplicity (35–48), is contrasted with the present Iron Age of Jove in which war prevails (49–52). Thoughts of his own death and epitaph (53–6) lead to a dream in which Venus leads him to an Elysium reserved for lovers (57–66), which is contrasted with a Tartarus reserved for the punishment of sinners against love (67–82). The poem ends with an appeal to Delia to remain faithful during his absence and with a description of his imagined happy home-coming to her (83–94).

The poet's skill is shown in the balance he achieves between these various themes and in the smooth transitions he forges between them.

3 *Phaeacia*: the name of the land Odysseus was shipwrecked on in *Odyssey* Books 6 and 7. It was identified by the Hellenistic Greek poet Callimachus with Corcyra (modern Corfu), an important military staging post on the way from Rome to the East. By using the mythological name Phaeacia, Tib. associates his own plight with that of Odysseus, an idea picked up at the end of the poem where Delia is linked with Penelope.

7–8 *dousing Syrian perfume | upon my ash*: when the funeral pyre had been extinguished the ashes would be doused in perfume, wine, and milk before being placed in an urn in a sepulchre.

11 *Three times*: see note to 1.2.56.

sacred lots: Delia consults lots drawn by a slave boy to divine whether Tib.'s journey will be safe.

18 *Saturn's holy day*: the first surviving mention in Latin literature of the Jewish Sabbath, our Saturday (Saturn's day). Many Jews came to Rome after the capture of Jerusalem by Pompey in 63 BC. Their strict observance of the Sabbath may have led Romans to consider it unlucky for important undertakings.

23 *Isis*: the cult of the Egyptian mother goddess, Isis, spread through the Mediterranean world in the Hellenistic age and reached Rome at the beginning of the first century BC. Attempts to restrict the cult in the twenties BC had little effect and it became particularly popular with women of Delia's class. The mistresses of Propertius and Ovid are also represented as her devotees. Her powers as a healing goddess were attested to by painted thank-offerings in her temples, cf. 27–8.

24 *bronze rattles*: the so-called sistrum used in the worship of Isis. The sound of the clashing metal was supposed to ward off evil spirits.

26 *nights of abstinence*: the periods of chastity offered to Isis, which usually lasted ten days (cf. Propertius 2.33.2) were a cause of concern for all the elegists.

30 *linen-clad*: linen, being a vegetable product, was considered purer than wool in the worship of Isis.

31 *unbound hair*: essential in all ancient religious and magical ceremonies.

twice each day: worship of Isis took place once before sunrise and once in the afternoon.

32 *on show among Pharian multitudes*: Delia's flowing locks would be conspicuous among the shaven heads of Isis's priests. Pharos (= Lighthouse), a small island off Alexandria, was one of the cult centres of Isis.

33 *Penates*: the traditional Roman gods of the household.

35 *Saturn's reign*: Saturn, whose name in Latin connects him with the sowing of crops, was originally an Etruscan deity. He was at an early stage equated with the Greek Chronos, father of Zeus, and ruler of the Golden Age. The traditional Golden Age of Saturn was a time when the earth spontaneously provided men with all their needs; there was consequently no need for agriculture, trade, travel, or war. Hence its relevance to Tib.'s current plight.

49 *With Jove now lord*: in contrast with the traditional Golden Age of Saturn, the present Iron Age of his son, Jove, is a time characterized by war and greed.

51–2 *false oaths ... impious slights*: the idea is that Tib.'s present suffering could result from divine anger. He asks for mercy on the grounds that he has not sworn falsely or committed sacrilege.

55–6 HERE LIES TIBULLUS ... LAND AND SEA: elegiac metre was the metre of the epitaph in real-life inscriptions. In the Hellenistic age these found their way into poetry. Epitaphs are embedded in the works of all three Roman elegists (cf. Propertius 2.13.35–6, 4.7.85–6, Ovid, *Amores* 2.6.61–2). Tib.'s is clearly intended as a compliment to his patron, Messalla. Unlike the epitaphs of his contemporaries in elegy, his contains no mention of his mistress or of his vocation as a love poet.

58 *Venus will lead me to Elysian fields*: the Elysian fields were the traditional home of dead warriors and heroes, who were led there by Hermes/ Mercury (see *Odyssey* 4.563–9). Tib.'s idea of a separate Elysium for lovers, led there by Venus, occurs here for the first time. Comparison with Propertius 4.7.59–69 suggests a lost common source for both in Greek poetry.

61 *Untilled land sprouts with cinnamon*: a clear parallel with the Golden Age of Saturn: cf. note to 35 and see lines 45–6.

66 *and sport their special myrtle in their tresses*: myrtle was sacred to Venus, the goddess of love.

67 *the Seat of Evil*: the reference is to Tartarus, the abode of the wicked after death.

69 *Tisiphone*: one of the three Erinyes, or Furies, who pursued sinners after death. Her name in Greek means 'Avenger of Bloodshed', which links her with the slaughter (49) of the Iron Age.

71 *Cerberus*: the monstrous guard dog of Hades, who prevented the shades from escaping. His head and neck bristle with snakes.

73 *Ixion*: mythical king of Thessaly, who attempted to rape Juno. He was punished in Tartarus by being fixed to a fiery wheel which revolved through eternity.

75 *Tityos*: a mythical giant, who tried to rape Leto. He was slain by Artemis and his body was stretched out as food for the vultures, who fed on his liver.

77 *Tantalus*: Tantalus was punished by never being able to quench his thirst. His crimes in most accounts concern either feeding the flesh of his son Pelops (see note to 1.4.64) to the gods, or stealing nectar and ambrosia from the gods to give to men. As all the other inhabitants of Tib.'s Tartarus had sinned against love, however, the crime hinted at here was probably his attempted rape of Jupiter's cup-bearer, Ganymede, which had apparently been related by the Hellenistic poet, Phanocles.

79 *the daughters of Danaus*: fifty in number. All but Hypermnestra sinned against Venus by murdering their husbands on their wedding night. Their punishment was to carry water forever in leaky vessels.

ELEGY 1.4

The poem consists of an elegant lecture on the art of pederasty delivered by the fertility god Priapus. It would be intended to shock and amuse the reader working through the collection in order, coming as it does after three love poems concerning Delia. The poem clearly inspired Ovid's later heterosexual *Art of Love*. It is the first of three poems (1.4, 1.8, 1.9) on the subject of Tib.'s love for the boy Marathus. Love of boys had formed part of the tradition of Greek lyric, elegy, and pastoral, but apart from one poem by Propertius (1.20) on the rape of Hylas, the topic is generally avoided by the other elegists, Propertius and Ovid (see Introduction, pp. xviii–xix).

Tib.'s request to Priapus for advice (1–6), leads, via a transitional couplet (7–8), into Priapus' lecture (9–72). Much of the lecture's humour is derived from the pompous, mock-didactic style of its delivery and from the rhetorical embellishment lent to its commonplace precepts. It is carefully structured in six sections: beware the attractions of boys (9–14); be patient (15–20); do not hesitate to use false oaths (21–6); do not delay too long (27–38); do whatever your boy wishes (39–56); the boys themselves should put poetry before money (57–72). As a twist in the tail we learn that the lecture was intended to be passed on by Tib. to a certain Titius (73). Titius' wife, however, will not let him make use of it (74). Consequently, Tib. himself will have to use the instructions provided to become a teacher of love (75–80). His position is further undermined at the end by the reflection that all this learning has not helped Tib. in his own affair with Marathus (81–4).

The theme of the 'teacher of love' on which the poem is based had occurred in Greek pastoral and Greek New Comedy (as reflected in their

Latin adaptations by Plautus) and becomes common in Roman elegy. In Ovid it becomes the basis for his mock-didactic *Art of Love* and *Remedy of Love*.

1 *Priapus*: see note to 1.1.17.

6 *Dog Star*: see note to 1.1.27.

7 *Bacchus' bucolic child*: Priapus was the son of Bacchus and Aphrodite (Venus).

25 *Dictynna*: a cult title of Artemis/Diana, as goddess of the hunt, meaning 'Lady of the Hunting Net'. Swearing by a god's favourite attributes, in this case Diana's hunting arrows, would normally make an oath more binding. Like Minerva, Diana was known for her virginity and chastity, and so there is humour in the idea that lovers would swear by either.

26 *Minerva*: an Italian goddess of handicraft, identified with the Greek Athena, and proud of her beautiful hair. Like Diana, she was known for her chastity.

32 *gates at Elis*: the starting gates used for horse-racing at the Olympic Games, held at Elis in the western Peloponnese.

37 *Phoebus and Bacchus*: the two male gods Phoebus (Apollo) and Bacchus balance the two female gods Diana and Minerva in 25–6. They were both known for their long hair and eternal youth.

63 *Nisus*: king of Megara, who had a purple lock of hair on which the safety of his city depended. His daughter Scylla cut it off and betrayed the city to her lover, the enemy commander, Minos of Crete. The story is mentioned frequently in both Latin and Greek literature.

64 *Pelops*: was dismembered and served as meat to the gods by his father Tantalus. The gods reassembled him as soon as they realized, but a shoulder had already been eaten by Ceres and an ivory replacement had to be substituted.

68 *Ops of Ida*: wife of Saturn, equivalent to the Greek Rhea, identified with Cybele, the Phrygian mother goddess of Mount Ida. Her chariot made a procession though the cities of the East accompanied by her priests, the castrated Galli.

70 *and hack vile parts to beats of Phrygia!*: at their initiation the priests of the Mother Goddess, Cybele, castrated themselves in a frenzy to the sound of the Phrygian flute.

73 *Titius*: this could be just a fictitious name, 'John Doe', especially as it is used in this way in Roman legal texts. For those in the know, however, it could refer to Marcus Titius, who succeeded Tib.'s patron Messalla in the consulship in 31 BC. He had recently married and this would give point to the mention of his wife in 74.

ELEGY 1.5

This is the second variant by Tib. on the song of the shut-out lover or *paraklausithyron* (for which see introductory note to Elegy 1.2), although the setting outside the mistress's door does not become clear until lines 67–8.

Tib. thought he could bear a separation, but now repents of his pride and is tortured by his love (1–4). He is willing to bear his punishment, but asks for forgiveness (5–8). His devotion had saved his mistress when she was ill, but a rival now enjoys her love (9–18). He had imagined an idyllic life for them in the country on her recovery, but now these dreams have been cast to the winds (19–36). He had tried unsuccessfully to find relief through wine and other women (37–40), who had blamed his impotence on Delia's witchcraft; but it was her beauty, not her magic spells, that had bewitched him (41–6). The real cause of his ruin had been an evil madam who had introduced Delia to a rich lover (47–58). Delia should reject the bawd's teaching and appreciate the advantages of a poor lover (59–66). Delia's door remains shut despite his song (67–8). He ends with a warning to Delia's current lover to beware of a rival, for even now a stranger is lurking at her door (67–76).

The elegy repeats a number of themes from 1.2, but these are given a different emphasis, reflecting a deterioration in the affair. The husband of 2.43 has been replaced by a rich lover, 5.47, introduced to Delia by a crafty madam. Tib. is now locked out not by the current lover, as in 1.2, but by Delia herself, who has become more mercenary in her choice of partners. The theme of the rustic idyll, still a possibility in 2.73–6, is expanded with more detail, 5.21–34, only to be shattered completely, 5.35–6. The witch, who had helped Tib. in 2.41–66, is replaced by the evil madam who leads Delia astray, 5.48–58. The threat of nemesis on the unidentified mocker outside her door at 2.89–98 has been replaced by a warning to Delia's current lover (5.69–76).

A reader coming to this poem from 1.4 could be tricked into thinking the separation mentioned in line 1 is between Tibullus and Marathus and the mention of the 'skilful lad' in 4 lends further weight to this mistaken impression. The connection between the end of 1.4 and the beginning of 1.5 is confirmed by a number of verbal echoes: *gloria*, 'pride' in 1.4.77 and 1.5.2; *torque(t)*, 'torture(s)' in 1.4.81 and 1.5.5; *parce quaeso*, 'spare me, please (I request)' in 1.4.83 and 1.5.7, and it is not until line 9 that the addressee's gender is revealed in the Latin as feminine. A similar piece of intentional misleading is to be found at the beginning of Elegy 1.8, where the reader is led into thinking the addressee of the beginning of the poem is a girl; not until line 23 is the real gender confirmed as male (see introductory note to 1.8).

5 *Torture and brand the beast*: Tib. refers to himself as 'the beast' in the third person. The reference is to burning and branding, typical slave punishments. As a slave of love, Tib. demands appropriate punishments for his wild rejection of love described in 1–2.

7–8 *but spare me . . . conjoined with mine!*: Tib.'s appeal for forgiveness is based on Hera's oath to Zeus in Homer, *Iliad* 15.39–40: 'by your own

sacred head and the couch of our wedded love'. By 'the head conjoined'
Tib. refers to Delia's head placed beside his on the couch in happier days.

14 *three times*: see note to 1.2.56.

20 *the god refused*: the unspecified god perhaps hints at Amor, the god of
love.

25 *a chatty servant boy*: the Latin for servant boy here is *verna*, literally 'a
house-born slave'. Such slaves born into the house appear to have been
treated more kindly and hence were more talkative and confident than
slaves bought from outside.

27 *the god of farmers*: probably Silvanus, see note to 1.1.14.

31 *Messalla*: Tib.'s patron, see note to 1.1.53.

36 *perfumed Armenia*: a remote province, mountainous and windy (cf. 35). It
exported perfumes which could have been the source of Delia's lover's
wealth.

45 *Thetis*: Thetis was a sea-nymph (Nereid), who, by the will of Zeus,
married Peleus of Thessaly and bore him a son, Achilles, who was
destined to be greater than his father. She is often represented in art as
riding on a bridled dolphin. Such mythological comparisons are com-
paratively rare in Tib. and this one represents a great compliment to
Delia. The main point of comparison is their beauty; though in many
versions of the story Thetis was an unwilling bride and this underlying
idea may hint at Tib.'s current difficulties with Delia.

47 *with a wealthy suitor near*: the rival of 17–18 is now revealed as a 'rich
lover' (*dives amator*). His presence is explained as a result of the influence
on Delia of a 'sneaky madam', or 'cunning procuress' (*callida lena*). The
blood-curdling curse on the procuress that follows (49–56) has the
effect of diverting blame from Delia herself, though she is criticized for
following her advice.

49–56 *May she consume ... from the crossroads!*: this curse on the bawd
occurs first here in Roman elegy and was then taken up by Propertius
(4.5.75–8) and Ovid (*Amores* 1.8.113–14). Tib. is introducing in mini-
ature a type of poem which existed as a full-blown literary form in earlier
Hellenistic Greek poetry, the curse poem.

52 *an owl*: owls were thought to portend death and disaster, particularly if
they sang from the roof.

55–6 *and run ... from the crossroads!*: having been forced by hunger to eat
bones left over by wolves, the bawd is to become a victim of lycanthropy,
wolf-madness, and is to howl through the town pursued by dogs. The
dogs are the hounds of Hecate (see note to 1.2.54), goddess of magic who
presides over crossroads.

57 *some god signals*: as often, the name of the god is not given. In this case it
is probably again Amor, the god of love (as at 20 above). The god who
protects lovers signs his agreement to Tib.'s curse.

67 *shut doors*: the setting of the poem as a shut-out lover's song is at last revealed.

70 *the fickle wheel of Fortune*: a Greek idea associated with the goddess Nemesis, reflecting the instability of good fortune. The lover who is in favour now will soon be out of favour and replaced by a rival (see 71–6, and R. Maltby, 'The Wheel of Fortune: Nemesis and the Central Poems of Tibullus I and II', in S. Kyriakidis and Francesco de Martino (eds.), *Middles in Latin Poetry* (Bari: Levante, 2005), 103–21).

76 *your small vessel drifts on current*: literally 'your skiff floats on running water'. The image suggests the instability of Delia's current lover's position. The current can sweep him away and he can be ousted. Similar images of the dangers of sailing applied to the vicissitudes of love occur in later elegy: cf. Propertius 2.4.19 and Ovid, *Amores* 2.4.7–8.

ELEGY 1.6

This is the final Delia poem of the collection. It is even more disillusioned than 1.5 and expresses the realization that love for Delia is not compatible with the rustic simplicity and traditional religious observance set out as Tib.'s ideal in 1.1. Now Delia is no longer separated from him against her will, as in 1.2 and 1.3, nor has she had a rich lover thrust on her by an evil bawd as in 1.5; rather she has taken a secret lover of her own accord, possibly the rival foreshadowed at the end of 1.5.

The poem opens (1–4) with an angry attack on the god of love. Amor is always leading him on, only to let him down. Delia has now taken a secret lover and uses against Tib. the very wiles he had taught her for use against her husband (5–14). In 15–24 Tib. addresses Delia's husband, advising him on how to stop her infidelities. He ends with the insolent suggestion that the husband should entrust her for safe-keeping to his own care. In 25–36 he lists the deceptions he has practised in the past against the husband, before repeating in more detail at 37–42 the proposal that he himself should be made Delia's guardian. A vivid description of the prophecy of Bellona's priestess that any rival who touches a girl under Love's protection should lose his wealth serves as a warning to potential rivals (43–54). He admits that Delia herself is not without blame (55), but prays that she be spared punishment for the sake of her mother, who had helped him in his affair (56–62). The poem ends with an appeal to Delia to remain faithful, backed up with a description of the miserable old age of the faithless woman (73–84). The final couplet (85–6) closes the whole Delia affair with the forlorn wish that the two of them should remain faithful into old age.

There is a coolness and distance in his relations with Delia which distinguish this poem from the rest of the cycle. Tib. realizes his trust in Delia has been misplaced and his contempt for her husband knows no bounds. There is irony in the knowledge that his own teaching is being used against him. The praise of Delia's mother is unparalleled in elegy and introduces a note of sentimentality which would not be found in Propertius or Ovid.

4–5 *trap . . . nets*: both hunting metaphors, picking up 'ensnared' in 1. In love poetry such metaphors are normally applied to the way the lover 'ensnares' his beloved. Tib. has transferred the imagery to the tricks played on him by the god of love in providing Delia with another lover.

6 *sly Delia*: the application of this adjective to Delia marks a hardening in his attitude to his mistress; cf. 'cheating girl' in line 15.

   someone: suggests the same person who was lurking outside Delia's door at the end of the previous poem, the 'someone' of 1.5.71. Thus Elegy 6 is linked to Elegy 5 in the same way as 5 was linked with 4 (see introductory note to 1.5).

8 *'husband'*: the Latin is *uir* 'man', which can apply either to a legal husband or simply to a current lover. This is the same as the man mentioned in 15, translated again 'husband', but referred to in Latin as *coniunx*, which has the same connotations as *uir*.

19–20 *nor fool you . . . send a signal*: for communication through nods and secret writing in wine on the table, cf. the lessons taught to lovers by Venus in 1.2.21–2.

22 *Good Goddess*: refers to Bona Dea, a Roman fertility goddess, whose rights were restricted to women. A visit to her temple is mentioned by Ovid in *Art of Love* 3.637–8 as a good way for a woman to give the slip to her guard.

24 *no fear about my eyes*: blinding was the punishment for men who attended the Bona Dea rites. As her altar would be outside the temple, if Tib. followed her only that far (see 23), he would not have committed sacrilege by entering the temple. The line of course would also bear the interpretation that Tib. has no fear of blinding as he knows Delia is not going to the temple.

27 *the victor*: a military image: Tib. was acting under love's orders. Cf. 30: 'Love was in charge', and note to 1.1.75.

33 *'wife'*: the Latin is *coniunx*, the same word that is applied to the 'husband' in 15 and with the same connotations of 'wife' or 'current mistress'.

38 *stripes . . . shackles*: for the image of the lover as slave to a mistress see note to 1.1.55. Tib. is the first to introduce servile beatings or 'stripes' in this context, though shackles are common.

39–40 *you who coif your hair . . . spacious folds*: excessive grooming of the hair and the wearing of loose togas characterized the kind of foppish Roman dandy who would be a threat to Delia's virtue.

41–2 *and let all . . . another road!*: the text of 42 is corrupt. The general meaning of the couplet must be that anyone who meets Tib. and Delia should keep their distance in order to avoid suspicion of attempting to make contact with her.

43 *A god himself*: must refer to the god of love, Amor; cf. 30 and 51.

45 *Bellona*: the Roman goddess of war, *bellum*, whose temple was on the Campus Martius. Her worshippers were notorious for their religious

frenzy. In Sulla's time she was identified with the Cappadocian Ma, whose temples were served by sacred prostitutes. Her priestesses would thus make suitable teachers of love. They, or more often Bellona's male priests, are known to have given prophecies while in a state of trance and to have slashed their arms and offered their blood to the worshippers or to the goddess.

56 *though if you're guilty*: the problem here is that the Latin *admitto* has a double sense and can mean either 'admit a lover' or 'commit a crime'. Both meanings are possibly present here. The translation 'if you are guilty' preserves this ambiguity. It may seem unlikely that Tib. would pray for leniency for Delia if she let in a lover, but he goes on to explain that he does this not for Delia, but for her mother's sake, who had helped them both in their affair.

57-8 *It's not for you . . . conquers rage*: the statement that Tib. wishes Delia to be spared not for her own sake but because of his regard for her mother is as much an insult to Delia as a compliment to her mother.

59-62 *She leads you . . . approaching feet*: two different situations involving the mother are described here. In 59-60 she leads Delia through the darkness to a rendezvous with Tib. In 61-2 the setting is the house of Delia's 'husband', and the mother listens out for Tib.'s footsteps and lets him in when he arrives.

67-8 *no headband . . . robe her feet*: Delia does not wear the braided hair and the long robe of the married matron. In 1.5.21-2 he may have imagined her as performing the duties of a traditional Roman wife on his country estate but in this last bitter poem he can remind her of her true social status. She may have a 'husband', but she is not married to him in the legal sense and although he wishes her to remain 'chaste', by which he means faithful to himself alone, she is certainly not married to Tib.

79 *ties the leashes to the rented loom*: the woman who remains true to no lover will lose her rich admirers in old age and have to weave to make a living on a rented loom. The 'leashes' (*licia*) are the vertical warp threads that are tied to the crossbeam of the loom. On Tib.'s use of technical language see R. Maltby, 'Technical Language in Tibullus', *Emerita* 67 (1999), 231-49.

85-6 *Let curses like these . . . white-haired lovers!*: although this is the last poem addressed to Delia, Tib. steps back from a final break in the last couplet and wishes that they should remain faithful lovers in old age. The wish proves a delusion and Delia is never mentioned again.

ELEGY 1.7

The elegy, written on the occasion of Messalla's birthday, celebrates his defeat of the Aquitanians, the triumph he was awarded for this on 25 September 27 BC, his mission to the East (Cilicia, Syria, Phoenicia, and Egypt) and his repair of the Via Latina. Beginning with the day of Messalla's birth, on which his future victories were foretold (1–4), the poem moves on to describe his triumph and his campaigns in Gaul (5–12). The central section of the poem is taken up with Messalla's mission to the East (13–22) and contains a hymn to the Egyptian god Osiris, who is identified with the life-giving Nile and the Classical wine god Bacchus (23–49). A concluding section (49–54) returns to the theme of Messalla's birthday with which the poem had started and Osiris and Messalla's birthday spirit (his Genius) are invited to attend. The elegy ends (55–64) with a series of good wishes addressed to Messalla and mention is made of the fame he continues to win from his repair of the Via Latina.

The poem has to be seen in the context of the recent civil wars between Antony and Octavian in which Egypt had been the base of Octavian's enemies Antony and Cleopatra. The defeat of Egypt had come as the climax of Octavian's own triumph in 29 BC, in which he celebrated his victory over Antony and Cleopatra at Actium in 31 BC. Egypt nevertheless remained a problem and in the same year as Messalla's triumph its governor, Cornelius Gallus (the inventor of Roman elegy), had been recalled by Octavian (known by this time as Augustus) for arrogance in the discharge of his duties and committed suicide in Rome. Here Tib.'s more positive portrayal of Egypt and her religion departs from contemporary Augustan propaganda and argues perhaps for the peaceful reintegration of this powerful province into the Roman world.

This is the first example of a developed Roman elegy from which the love theme is almost entirely absent.

2 *the Parcae*: the Roman equivalent of the Greek Fates, the Moirai, Clotho who spins, Lachesis who twists, and Atropos who cuts the thread of each human's life. As they spun the threads of a man's life they knew everything that would happen to him, and so could predict his future in their song.

3 *the tribes of Aquitaine*: these tribes occupied the south-western corner of Gaul, bounded by the Pyrenees, the bay of Biscay, and the river Garonne.

4 *Atur*: the manuscripts read Atax, now the modern river Aude, which in fact flows well to the east of Aquitania, in Gallia Narbonensis. Most scholars correct the reading to *Atur,* the river Adour, which would have flowed in south-west Aquitania.

5–8 *So it has happened . . . chariot*: in these four lines Tib. sketches the main ingredients of a Roman triumph: the spectators, the shackled captives, and the victorious general crowned with laurel and riding in a gleaming white chariot. The date of Messalla's triumph is firmly dated by the inscriptional evidence of the *Fasti Triumphales* (*Corpus Inscriptionum Latinarum* 1^2, p. 180) to 25 September 27 BC.

9 *no prize without me*: Tib. is proud to mention his own contribution to the campaign, despite his anti-military stance elsewhere.

Santonican shores: named from the Santoni (from whom are named modern Saintonges and Saintes), who were a Celtic tribe living between the Charente and the Garonne.

10 *Tarbelli's Pyrenees*: the western Pyrenees, named from the Aquitanian tribe the Tarbelli, who gave their name to modern Tarbes.

11–12 *Arar . . . Rhodanus . . . Garunna . . . Liger*: the Latin names for the rivers Saône, Rhone, Garonne, and Loire respectively.

12 *Carnutes*: a Celtic tribe living between the Seine and the Loire, who gave their name to modern Chartres.

13 *Cydnus*: Tibullus now moves on to Messalla's tour of the East, beginning with a mention of the river Cydnus, which rises in Mount Taurus and flows through Tarsus. It was the main river of Cilicia, a Roman province in modern Turkey. Messalla's visit to the East took place some time after the battle of Actium in 31 BC and before his triumph in 27 BC.

15 *Taurus*: the ancient Mount Taurus is now known as Dagh, in Turkey. In ancient times it was cultivated to its summit, which rises to over 3,000 metres.

17 *white doves revered by Syrians*: white doves were sacred to the Syrian goddess, Astarte, as they were to her Greek counterpart Aphrodite.

19 *Tyre*: the city was built on an island off the coast of Palestine and was famous for its high towers. Tib. in these lines could be suggesting an etymological link between Tyre and *turris*, 'tower'. The Phoenicians, whose city it was, are supposed to have invented navigation by the stars.

21 *Sirius*: the Dog Star, whose rising shortly after the summer solstice portended intense heat (see note to 1.1.27).

23–4 *in what lands . . . hid your head from sight*: an allusion to the ancient conundrum of the source of the Nile and its floods.

27 *the Memphis Bull*: the bull, called Apis, was supposed by the ancient Egyptians to be an incarnation of their god Osiris. It had a splendid temple at Memphis. On its death the whole country mourned until a new bull was found.

29–38 *With skilful hands . . . settled rhythms*: praise of Osiris as the inventor of agriculture. In the Greek tradition the invention of the plough was ascribed to Demeter or Triptolemus, and the discovery of the vine to Bacchus. Praise of a god as a first inventor is a traditional hymnic feature. The identification of Osiris with Bacchus (Dionysus) goes back in the Greek tradition as least as far as Herodotus, *Histories* 2.42.

42 *sturdy shackles*: Bacchus brings relief even to slaves. The reference here could be to the chained slave-gangs who worked the fields of the Roman aristocracy.

46 *golden robes*: in Greek iconography Bacchus was associated with a long saffron-coloured robe. According to Plutarch a similar robe was used in Egypt to drape statues of Osiris.

47 *finery from Tyre*: i.e. robes of Tyrian purple. Tyre was the centre for the manufacture of purple dye from a vein found in various species of shellfish. Cloth so dyed became a symbol of power and luxury in the ancient world (see note to 1.2.77).

48 *baskets holding sacred secrets*: baskets of wickerwork contained the sacred objects of the god's mystery cult. Such baskets figured in the worship of Bacchus, Isis, and Osiris. For the cult of Bacchus in Italy see A. J. North's article *Bacchanalia* in the *Oxford Classical Dictionary*, 3rd edn, revised (Oxford University Press, 2003).

49 *Genius*: each Roman had a guardian spirit called his Genius, who was born with him and protected him during his lifetime. Sacrifices to a statue of the Genius were particularly appropriate on one's birthday (see note to 2.2.5).

54 *Mopsopian sweet honeycakes*: offerings of cakes were made to the gods on special occasions, particularly on one's birthday (cf. 2.2.8). Cakes offered to Bacchus were mixed or coated with honey, of which the most prestigious kind came from Mount Hymettus near Athens, hence Mopsopian here from Mopsopus, a mythical king of Attica.

55 *your heirs*: Messalla's elder son Messallinus, whose induction to a priestly college is to be the subject of Elegy 2.5, was certainly alive at the time the present poem was written.

57 *your landmark road*: a reference to the programme of road repair and building undertaken by Augustus and his generals after the civil wars and paid for by the spoils of victory. Messalla was assigned part of the Via Latina between Tusculum and Alba Longa.

58 *white homes*: a play on the name of Alba, which means 'white' in Latin, possibly referring to the white villas that were characteristic of the area (cf. Horace, *Epodes* 1.29, who refers to a 'gleaming villa' close to Tusculum). There may also be a veiled reference to Tib.'s own name Albius Tibullus.

59–60 *since there . . . fitting skill*: the couplet refers to the two main stages of road building: spreading the hard gravel base and then fitting the paving stones over the top. As a serving soldier Tib. could have witnessed these operations at first hand.

63 *Birth-Spirit*: the Latin is *Natalis*, a word used of a man's Genius (see note to 49 above) on the occasion of his birthday; cf. 2.2.1.

ELEGY 1.8

Tib. assumes the role of a teacher of love (1–6); cf. 1.4. But the addressee of his advice is kept dark until line 23. At 6–7 the person addressed is asked to admit to being in love and in 9–14 they are warned of the uselessness of cosmetics. In 15–16 the addressee is contrasted with a certain girl who pleases, though she does not use make-up. All this discussion of make-up and hairstyle and the contrast with a girl in 15–16 suggests at first that Tib. is giving his lecture to a girl, but with the words in 23 'why whine spells harm a wretched lad' it becomes clear that he is addressing a boy (see introductory note to 1.5 for similar misleading information about the gender of the addressee). The point is that it is not magic (17–23) but physical contact (24–6) that has made him fall in love. It now becomes clear that the girl mentioned in 15–16 was the girl the boy loves. It is to her that Tib. now turns in 27 with 'You must remember . . . ' and advises her to be kind to the boy and to ask for gifts only from ageing lovers (27–34). Venus can give advice on affairs with young men (35–8). Riches can bring no pleasure to a loveless woman in old age (39–42); old age is the time to use make-up (43–6). Youth should be used for love before it slips away (47–8). Lines 49–54 provide a bridge passage leading into the boy's speech at 55, who is identified for the first time as Marathus in 49. The girl should spare him, as he is sick with love for her, and be harsh only on her old lovers. Lines 55–66 consist of a direct address from Marathus to the girl, giving advice on love's secrets, but admitting in 61, as Tib. had done at the end of 1.4, that in his own case his arts fail him. In a concluding section, 67–78, Tib. addresses the boy and girl alternately. The boy should stop crying and the girl, now named as Pholoe (69), is warned her pride could incur divine displeasure. Marathus once made fools of his lovers but now hates being shut out by them. Pholoe should learn the same lesson.

The dramatic form of this elegy, in which Tib. imagines he has a pair of lovers in front of him and addresses each in turn, as well as giving a speech to Marathus, is reminiscent of drama and may have its roots in Roman New Comedy or mime. Of course Tib. is no impartial observer. He himself was one of Marathus' former lovers and his emphasis on the boy's youthful good looks and lack of success with Pholoe could be an attempt to get him back by suggesting that Marathus is not yet ready for an affair with a girl.

3–4 *lots . . . livers . . . songbirds*: the reference is to three methods of divination: sortilege (use of lots, cf. 1.3.11–12), haruspicy (examination of the liver and entrails of sacrificial animals), and augury (observation of the flight and call of birds). All three occur again at 2.5.11–14.

5–6 *Venus herself . . . floggings*: for Venus as a teacher of love see 1.2.19–24. Tib. perhaps sees himself as a slave of love who is bound and beaten by Venus into knowledge, though the reference to sacred knots in 5 suggests some form of mystery cult.

7 *A god*: probably Amor again. The addressee attempts to make his feet appear small by tightening the loop of his sandal. Large feet were thought ugly in both men and women, so Tib. does not reveal their gender by this reference.

21–2 *A spell . . . clanging cymbals*: the spell for drawing down the moon from the sky was called the Thessalian trick. Thessaly was the traditional home of witches. The clashing symbols are used to ward off evil magic: see note to 1.3.24.

23 *a wretched lad*: the first indication the addressee of the first half of the poem was a boy.

27 *You must remember*: with these words Tib. turns to address the girl Marathus loves, mentioned in 15–16, and later revealed as Pholoe (69).

44 *unripe nutshells*: Pliny's *Natural History* 15.87 tells us the green outer skin of the walnut produced a reddish hair-dye.

46 *slack skin . . . new look*: Pliny's *Natural History* 24.43 mentions mastic gum and Juvenal 6.462 a dough plaster for tightening loose skin and removing wrinkles.

49 *No torturing Marathus!*: recalls the way Marathus 'tortured' Tib. at 1.4.81.

50 *be tough on ancient greybeards!*: recalls the advice of 29 above.

51 *He has no medical defence*: the reference is to a grave illness *sontica causa* that would provide a valid excuse for not appearing in court, hence 'medical defence'. Marathus has nothing more serious than love-sickness.

55 *'Why scorn me?'*: here Tib. reports a speech by Marathus addressed to Pholoe.

67–8 *Stop crying, lad! . . . your tears!*: addressed by Tib. to Marathus.

69–78 *I'm warning you . . . with prayers!*: addressed by Tib. to Pholoe. The name Pholoe is also found of a harsh girl in Horace, *Odes* 1.33.9, addressed significantly to an Albius, i.e. Tibullus.

ELEGY 1.9

Like 1.8, with which it forms a close pair, the elegy consists of an address by Tib. to two characters. In this case they are both unnamed. One is a boy, with whom Tib. is in love (presumably Marathus). The second is an old married man who has bought the boy's love with gifts. Three unnamed female characters are also mentioned: a young girl, whose affair with Marathus Tib. has furthered, the old man's wife, and the old man's drunken sister. It would lend a certain economy and piquancy to the pair of poems if the old man was the 'grey-haired' lover of 1.8.29, and if his wife and the young man's mistress were the same person, namely Pholoe of 1.8.69.

The theme of retribution with which the previous poem ends (1.8.77–8) opens the present elegy, with a warning to the boy that punishment will eventually catch up with him for breaking his promises to Tib. (1–4). The abrupt line of thought in 5–16 reflects Tib.'s mixed feelings of anger and continued love for the boy. A plea for mercy (5–6) is interrupted by various illustrations of human greed (7–10), leading (11) to the charge against the boy that he has been seduced by gifts and to a request for appropriate punishments (12–16). Tib. recalls his past warnings to the boy about accepting bribes and the boy's false assurances that he would not do so (17–38). Another abrupt change of direction at 39–40 introduces the figure of the boy's mistress, who should be as cruel to the boy as he is to Tib. Tib. had helped them in their affair, but now regrets it (41–6) as he regrets the praises he had sung of the boy (47–50). A single harsh couplet dismisses the boy for his greed (51–2) and at 53 Tib. turns to address the old seducer: may his wife have frequent affairs and surpass his sister in licentiousness (53–64); he is too stupid to notice his wife's affair with a young lover (65–74). Finally Tib. turns again to Marathus, asking how he could have taken money to sleep with such a monster (75–8). The end of the poem closes the Marathus affair (79–84): Marathus will suffer when he sees Tib. taking a new lover and Tib will dedicate a palm to Venus in thanks for his escape from Marathus.

The elegy belongs to a well-recognized type in ancient poetry: the poem announcing the end of an affair. The poet's detached stance of the 'teacher of love' in 1.8 is abandoned and replaced by that of a naïve lover whose feelings of love, anger, and resentment are fully engaged. The poem serves as an illustration of the point made first at the end of the mock-didactic 1.4 (lines 81–2) and repeated here in Marathus' case at 1.8.61, that abstract teaching is of no help when it comes to a real-life affair.

7–10 *For cash ... ruled by wind*: the transition to the profit motive is abrupt. The two illustrations chosen, farming and seafaring, are those which in 1.3.37–42 are described as absent from the Golden Age, a time characterized by the absence of greed.

11 *a god*: another vague reference to the god of love, Amor, as also at 24, 25, 27.

12 *to ash and streaming water!*: chosen because they are quickly dispersed. Compare 1.6.53–4 where the man who violates a girl under love's protection is to have his wealth flow away like blood and ash.

13–16 *Soon he will pay ... pampered feet*: the point appears to be that the boy will lose his beauty by accompanying a rich lover on a long, hot journey. This is a reversal of 1.4.41–2 where the lover of boys is advised to put up with similar hardships in pursuit of his love.

15 *His beauty will be scorched*: boys and mistresses should ideally be pale. A sunburnt complexion was associated with peasants and frowned upon.

21–2 *attack my flesh ... brand my head, | and slash my shoulders*: all traditional slave punishments, which Tib. would prefer to suffer as a slave lover of Marathus, than to see Marathus sell himself. For love as slavery (*servitium amoris*) see note to 1.1.56.

33–4 *farmland in Campania ... Falernum's fields*: Campania was a volcanic plain in central Italy, noted for its fertility. In the north of this area lay Falernum, noted for its high-quality Falernian wine.

41–2 *so no words were heard ... at night?*: Tib. recalls how he accompanied Marathus with a torch (another servile task) on his late-night meetings with Pholoe, and presumably acted as look-out, so that they were not seen or overheard.

43–4 *as my gift ... behind closed doors*: the phrase 'behind closed doors' must refer to a scene at Pholoe's house. Marathus appears and loses hope of seeing her, but after an intervention by Tib. (hence 'as my gift') she comes veiled to the door and hides behind it until the coast is clear.

49 *Vulcan*: the fire-god, standing here by metonymy for fire.

53 *But as for you*: having dismissed Marathus, Tib. now turns to his ageing seducer.

59 *your frisky sister*: Tib. does not specify whose the sister is, but it would
   be more to the point and more insulting if it were the old seducer's rather
   than his wife's.

70 *robe from Tyre?*: the reference is to a robe dyed in Tyrian purple (see
   note to 1.2.77). Like the golden bracelets in 69 this would be a sign of
   extreme luxury.

82 *a golden palm*: a symbol of victory, often dedicated to Jupiter by victorious
   generals. Tib.'s victory is his release from his love for Marathus, and thus
   he dedicates it to the goddess of love. The act may also symbolize his
   retirement (if only temporarily) from love, as soldiers often hung up their
   arms in dedication to a god on retirement.

83–4 *TIBULLUS ... GRATITUDE*: the elegiac metre was in real life used
   in dedicatory inscriptions, so such mock dedicatory inscriptions become
   a common elegiac motif; cf. 1.2.99–100, Propertius 2.14.27–8, Ovid,
   Amores 1.11.27–8.

ELEGY 1.10

After the rejection of Delia in 1.6 and Marathus in 1.9 the theme of the poet's
own love is replaced by the old Roman ideal of family life with children. As is
appropriate for the concluding poem of the book, the elegy recalls a number of
themes of the opening poem. Both poems reject war as based on greed and
praise simple piety and a peaceful rustic existence. However, whereas in
1.1 Tib. appears to have had the choice of rejecting war, in the present poem
he is being dragged off to war against his will. The poem shares with 1.3 the
realization that the idyllic existence he had longed for in 1.1 is not possible in
the modern age. The only hope for Tib.'s ideal is not through help provided
to him as an individual in response to his prayers but through the restoration
of peace to society in general; hence the central importance of the invocation
to personified Peace.

The poem begins with a curse on the inventor of war (1–4), which is
motivated by greed and was absent in simpler, more pious times (5–10). Tib.
wishes he had been born then; as it is, he is being dragged off to war (11–14).
His appeal to his ancestral Lares to save him is backed up by a description of
the traditional piety of men of old and of his own piety in the present day,
which is to be preferred to military glory (15–32). A description of the horrors
of untimely death in war (33–8) is balanced by a description of the contented
old age of the rustic (39–43). An invocation to Peace as the inventor of
agriculture (45–50) is interrupted by a passage rejecting amatory violence
after a rustic festival in favour of more gentle conduct (59–65). The poem ends
on an emphatic repetition of the invocation to Peace (67–8).

1–4 *Who was the first ... death were opened*: a variant on the traditional
   curse on the first inventor.

2 *ired and truly iron*: attempts to bring out the verbal play in the Latin of
   ferus et vere ferreus 'fierce and truly made of iron'. The word *ferus* 'fierce'

also prepares the way for *feras* 'wild beasts' in 6 and the idea that weapons were intended originally only as protection against wild beasts. The word *ferreus* 'made of iron' reflects the man's invention of the iron sword, for which the Latin was *ferrum*, 'an iron'.

7–8 *Gold riches ... sacred feasts*: for riches as the cause of war, cf. 1.1.1–2. The idea goes back at least as far as Plato, *Phaedo* 66c: 'it is in order to get money that all wars are made.'

10 *mottled ewes*: probably a reference to spotted sheep, whose wool was less valuable, emphasizing the simple poverty of ancient times.

12 *sad wars*: the Latin phrase *tristia arma* specifically suggests civil wars. The phrase recurs in 52, 'mournful weapons'.

trumpet: the war trumpet; cf. note to 1.1.4.

13 *I'm dragged to war now*: we have no indication of what campaign Tib. refers to here. It could be his first, as his appeal to the Lares in 15–16 mentions only their protection of him in childhood and not on previous campaigns. Poems in a collection did not appear in chronological order of composition.

15 *Lares*: see note to 1.1.19. Children were under their special protection, and as a child at home Tib. would have run about beneath their image.

19 *a wooden god*: i.e. the Lar.

21–2 *He was appeased ... sacred head*: offerings of first fruits were made to the Lar. In 1.1.13–16 similar offerings were made to Silvanus and to Ceres.

25 *turn bronze javelins away from me*: the protection of the Lares extended to war; cf. Propertius 3.3.11.

26–7 *and as I brace ... ancestral fields*: these two verses are supplied by the translator to fill a lacuna in the Latin.

29 *I'll follow in clean clothes*: a clean white robe was worn to denote ritual purity at the ceremony. The same phrase is used again in the same context at 2.1.13.

29–30 *the basket bound | with myrtle leaves*: a rush basket was used to contain the sacred objects for the ceremony. Myrtle was a suitable offering to the Lar, but it is normally associated with the love goddess, Venus, and so it is appropriate for an offering from a love poet. It serves to contrast him with the soldier of 31–2, whose patron god is Mars, the god of war.

33–4 *so as ... upon the table*: the returning soldier boasts of his exploits and paints his camp in wine on the table while Tib. quietly drinks. The idea of writing in wine on the table had occurred earlier in 1.6.19–20 in an amatory context.

38 *Cerberus*: see note to 1.3.71.

Styx's filthy oarsman: Charon, who on payment of a coin ferried the souls of the dead across the Styx. He was notorious for his squalor and ugliness; cf. Virgil, *Aeneid* 6.298–9: 'the horrible ferryman Charon, frightful in his squalor'.

40 *with shredded cheeks and smoking hair*: the dead behave like Roman mourners, scratching their cheeks in grief (cf. note to 1.1.67–8). They also retain traces of the funeral pyre, hence 'smoking hair' (see note to 2.6.39–40).

47–52 *may Peace . . . mournful weapons*: a eulogy to deified Peace. The goddess had been depicted on the coins of Julius Caesar and, in the East, of Augustus and represented internal concord, free from civil war. Here she is given many of the attributes of the corn goddess, Ceres, with whom she was associated in Augustan propaganda. As inventor of agriculture Peace also shares many of the functions of Osiris in 1.7.29–38 and the gods of the countryside in 2.1.37–42.

51–2 *With Peace . . . mournful weapons*: the association of Peace with glittering farm implements but rusting weapons goes back ultimately to Homer: cf. *Odyssey* 16.284ff. and 19.4ff. It is later used by Ovid in *Fasti* 4.927–8.

52 *mournful weapons*: as at 12 above the Latin *tristia arma* suggests civil wars.

53 *A farmer, barely sober*: the transition to the farmer is somewhat abrupt and a couplet may have dropped out before it.

54 *from the grove*: a sacred grove, used for religious festivals, at which the farmer has become drunk.

55 *the wars of Venus*: the theme of love as war (*militia amoris*) again; see note to 1.1.75.

59–60 *playful Love . . . angry couple*: Love urges his warriors on to fight as in 1.3.64, but once he has roused them he sits between them unmoved, an image inspired perhaps by a painting.

69–70 *So come . . . resplendent breast!*: a return to the theme of 47–52. The appeal to Peace with which the poem ends recalls the prayer to Venus at the end of Elegy 1.2. The image of fruit flowing from her breast could have been inspired by her depiction on coins or in paintings.

BOOK TWO

ELEGY 2.1

The second book opens with a dramatization of a rustic festival in which the poet himself takes on the leading role. The festival in question is probably the *lustratio agri* or *Ambarvalia*, a ritual walking of the field boundaries. This was followed by a sacrifice intended to increase the productivity of the fields and livestock.

An initial proclamation of the holiday (1–14) is followed by a description of the procession to the altar of the sacred lamb (15–16). There is a prayer to the ancestral gods (17–24), followed by an acknowledgement that the omens of the sacrifice are favourable (25–6). During the customary drinking that follows a toast is proposed to Messalla in his absence (27–36). A prayer to the rustic gods, relating their role in the development of civilization (37–66), leads into an account of the power of Cupid (67–80), who is invited to join in the feast at the end of the festival (81–90). The poem, like a number of Virgil's *Eclogues*, begins with the morning and ends with nightfall.

Tib.'s own sufferings in love are suggested in 70, but there is no mention of the new mistress, Nemesis, who is not named until 2.3.55; a surprising omission from the book's programmatic first poem. As a daughter of Night, it is possible Nemesis is hinted at in the mention of the murky Dreams, also daughters of Night, with which the poem ends (90).

1 *Be quiet, everyone!*: a ritual appeal for silence at the beginning of a religious ceremony.

3–4 *Bacchus . . . Ceres*: as the male and female gods who provide the staples of wine and corn respectively this pair of deities is often linked. Bacchus is frequently portrayed with bull's horns as a symbol of animal strength and vitality. Ceres' crown of corn spikes was mentioned earlier at 1.1.16.

5 *in sacred light*: i.e. on a sacred day; 'light' is used metonymically here for 'day', as often in Latin poetry of this period.

9 *Let everything be for the gods*: i.e. normal agricultural activity should be suspended in favour of service to the gods.

13 *The gods are pleased by abstinence*: for this idea of ritual celibacy cf. 1.3.25–6.

19 *May cornfields not elude the harvest with sly stalks*: the metaphor is taken from cheating or eluding one's opponent in a gladiatorial contest. The prayer is that the cornfields should not cheat the harvest with young shoots that do not fulfil their promise, hence 'sly stalks'.

22–4 *pile large logs . . . and play*: the reference seems to be to making a bonfire and building shelters as part of an outdoor festival.

27–8 *smoked Falernian . . . Chian*: Falernian was a strong wine (see note to 1.9.33–4) which improved with age. The casks, which were dated by the year of the consul in which they were produced, were stored in a smoky place, often in the roof, to aid maturation. Chian wine was of a lighter kind, and was often mixed with the stronger Falernian.

32 *absent person's name!*: Tib. skilfully introduces the name of his patron, Messalla, to the programmatic first poem of the book. As a member of the priestly Arval Brotherhood he may have been absent in Rome celebrating in an urban context the same rustic festival that Tib. attends in the country.

33 *Aquitaines*: for Messalla's triumph over Aquitania, see introductory note to 1.7.

37–66 *I praise the farm*: Tib. sings a hymn (ll. 37–66) in praise of the rustic gods as promoters of civilization. This is the same role as that attributed to Osiris in 1.7.29–48.

47–8 *the scorching star | of heaven*: i.e. the Dog Star (see note to 1.1.27).

52 *metrically*: there is a pun here in the Latin words *certo . . . pede* which can either mean 'with a sure foot' or 'in a fixed metre'.

53 *once he ate*: the Latin *satur*, 'satiated' with wine and food, hints etymologically at the rustic songs being the origin of 'satire'.

55 *Bacchus . . . daubed himself with cinnabar*: gods were regularly painted red (see 1.1.17), especially for ceremonial occasions. But here the reference may have been to the red wine lees, *tryges* in Greek, with which actors in tragedy were supposed to have smeared their faces. For the connection between Bacchus and tragedy see note to 57.

57 *a most worthy prize—the goat*: another etymological hint at the connection between Bacchus and tragedy. Tragic actors were awarded a goat, *tragos* in Greek, as a prize for their songs, which were performed for Bacchus (Dionysus). The goat was an appropriate sacrifice to the god of vines, as it could destroy them by its grazing.

60 *Lares*: see note to 1.1.19.

63 *stint*: the amount of wool to be spun into yarn in an allotted time.

66 *as weights bang*: terracotta weights were used to keep the warp tight and banged together when the comb, which presses the weft threads together, was brought down.

70 *OH MY*: an oblique reference to Tib.'s own sufferings in love.

75–6 *With him as guide . . . to her lad*: Cupid's help to the girl in love parallels the help provided by Venus for lovers in 1.2.17ff. Both passages are characterized by military imagery (cf. sentries here).

83–4 *call him for the herds . . . yourselves*: calling Cupid to the herds to promote their reproduction is a regular part of the rustic festival. But the human participants also call upon him to help them in their own love affairs, softly at first (84) and then out loud, hence 'bellow' (85). Ritual purity before the festival has given way to ribald merriment after it.

87–90 *Night yokes horses . . . spectral feet*: the description of Night and her attendants with which the poem ends could have been suggested by a painting. The stars, sleep, and dreams were traditionally the daughters of Night. So was Nemesis, the dark mistress who presides over the second book.

ELEGY 2.2

Like 1.7 this is a birthday poem, in this case addressed to Tib.'s friend, Cornutus, who is also the addressee of Elegy 2.3. Whereas in 1.7 the birthday of Messalla provided the occasion for a poem on his triumph, here the birthday of Cornutus is the starting point for a poem predicting his marriage (11–22). We are to imagine Cornutus engaged to a girl he would like to marry; the birthday would provide a suitably auspicious occasion for the marriage to take place. An inscription in Rome dated to 21 or 20 BC (*Corpus Inscriptionum Latinarum* 6.323338) mentions Cornutus with Messalla as a member of a priestly college, the Arval Brothers. His full name is M. Caecilius M.f. Gal. Cornutus. He probably served with Messalla in the camp of the liberators after the death of Julius Caesar, and inscriptional evidence also connects him with Messalla's trip to the East in 30 BC, which was the background to Elegy 3.1. The forthcoming marriage, mentioned in the second half of the poem, could possibly have linked Cornutus with Messalla's family.

Like 2.1 this is a dramatic elegy in which Tib. performs the role of master of ceremonies. The opening echoes the first couplet of the previous poem in its appeal for ritual silence (1-2). Cornutus' Genius, probably in the form of a statue, is to attend the ceremony and witness the burning of incense and the offering of gifts in his honour (3-8). Tib. asks the Genius to grant Cornutus' wishes and when he sees the Genius nod, he asks Cornutus to make his request (9-10). Tib. prophesies that Cornutus will ask for a wife's faithful love (11-12), which he will prefer to all the riches of the world (13-16). When Cornutus makes his prayer Tib. requests Amor to come flying down bringing with him the golden bonds of a stable marriage (17-20). In the last couplet the birthday and wedding themes are combined when Tib. asks the Birthday Spirit to provide Cornutus with offspring in the future.

1 *Birth-Spirit*: see note to 1.7.63.

5 *Genius*: see note to 1.7.49. His image would be carried from the shrine of the Lares within the house to the scene of the birthday ceremonies. The apparent nodding of assent by the Genius in 10 would not then be pure fantasy.

11 *a wife's true love*: Tib. prophesies that Cornutus will pray to be married to a loyal wife.

17 *Prayers tumble out*: i.e. from Cornutus' lips. He finally makes his prayer.

on beating wings: winged Amor or Cupid was a familiar figure in the art and poetry of the time.

18 *wedlock's golden bonds*: the image of the bonds of love is connected with Amor (Love) again in 2.4.4 and with Venus in 1.2.92. They are described as *flava*, 'golden' or, more literally, 'saffron' in this case, as saffron was the colour associated by the Romans with the marriage ceremony.

22 *frolic at your feet*: the reference is to crowds of children playing around the foot of the Genius's statue.

ELEGY 2.3

This elegy is the first in a series of poems concerned with the new, dark and mercenary mistress of Book 2, Nemesis. Whereas the countryside had been seen as an ideal background to Tib.'s affair with Delia, the natural setting for his affair with Nemesis is the city (see 58, 69). The countryside has become a harsh place of realistic labour that keeps him from his mistress. Wealth, gained through war, had been rejected in Book 1, but now, after an initial diatribe against it (41–54), Tib. declares himself willing to espouse it, if it will forward his affair with Nemesis (55–64).

The structure is as follows. Tib.'s mistress is being detained in the country-side, where the love gods have followed her (1–4). He would be willing to do hard labour in the countryside simply to be with her (5–10). Even Apollo sacrificed his good looks, his poetry and oracles to work for his lover Admetus in the country in the old days when gods were not ashamed to serve Venus openly (11–36). Tib. addresses his rival with an attack on the greed of the present age (37–54). But since girls prefer wealth he is willing to provide Nemesis with luxuries she can parade in the city (55–64). However, he has been replaced in Nemesis' affections by an ex-slave (65–6). Ceres and Bacchus are cursed for keeping Nemesis in the country (67–72). Life was better in pre-agricultural days, when men fed on acorns and dressed in skins but love was free (73–80). Fine clothes are useless in the absence of a mistress (81–4); better to serve her as a chained slave on her country estates (85–6).

The mythological excursus on Apollo's love for Admetus (11–36) and even the diatribe against loot (41–54) are unique in Tib. and look forward to the style of Ovid, who as a young man of 20 could well have been present at the first recital of this poem.

1 *Cornutus*: the initial address to Cornutus (see introductory note to 2.2), who has no further role in the poem, provides a link with 2.2, and invites a contrast between Cornutus' married love and Tib.'s affair with an unsuitable new mistress.

9 *sunlight burns my slender limbs*: on the association of sunburn with peasants see note to 1.9.15.

10 *blisters*: the town dweller's hands would be soft and liable to blisters (cf. 1.4.48).

11 *Apollo fed the cattle of Admetus*: Admetus was the king of Pherae in Thessaly. Apollo, the god of poetry, performed menial tasks in the country to win over his mortal lover, just as Tib. is willing to humiliate himself by working in the country in the proximity of his beloved. In both cases personal appearance and artistic accomplishments are insufficient to attract the object of love. On the role of service (*obsequium*) in pursuit of love, cf. 1.4.39–52.

14 *Love overcame his skill at medicine*: the idea that love is a disease impervious to medicine is a common one in ancient poetry. There is an added piquancy here in the fact that Apollo was a god of medicine (cf. Ovid, *Metamorphoses* 1.521).

16 *it's said . . . worked*: this line is added by the translator to fill a lacuna (of uncertain length) in the manuscripts.

17–20 *and taught techniques . . . for making whey*: there is humour in applying to the trivial art of cheese-making language more appropriate to Apollo's achievements in areas such as poetry, prophecy, and medicine.

22 *his sister blushed*: Apollo's sister was the huntress Diana.

25–6 *In crisis ... from the shrines*: Apollo neglects his duties as god of prophecy.

27 *Latona*: Apollo's mother, the Latin equivalent of the Greek Leto.

28 *even his stepmother*: Juno, wife of Apollo's father Jupiter. Stepmothers were traditionally supposed to be harsh, hence 'even'.

30 *Phoebus*: one of the names of Apollo.

31 *Delos ... Delphic Pytho*: a reference to Apollo's two great shrines at Delos (his birthplace) and Delphi (his chief residence). Pytho was the name of the district round Delphi and was derived from the serpent Python that Apollo slew there.

35–6 *scandal ... scandal*: the Latin *fabula* means 'byword', 'scandal' here, as at 1.4.83, where it is translated as 'shameful joke'.

37 *But you*: Tib. turns to address his rich rival.

38 *must camp out*: a military image, with Cupid as a stern general giving orders.

39–40 *be mindful ... your prize*: this couplet is supplied by the translator to fill a lacuna in the manuscripts.

46 *beaks for rocking vessels*: iron beaks were added to galleys for use like battering rams in naval engagements. The warships that resulted would have been rather unstable at sea.

51 *He hems in open seas with walls*: artificial saltwater fish-ponds were constructed by shutting off a portion of the sea with a concrete wall. Such fish-ponds were considered the height of extravagance.

53–4 *jugs from Samos ... cups | from Cumae's wheels*: Samian and Cumaean pottery, being home-produced, was relatively inexpensive and here represents modest, as opposed to extravagant, living.

57 *Nemesis*: the delayed naming of the mistress achieves its maximum effect by being linked to a context of wealth and urban living. The literal meaning, 'retribution', is very much to the point here, representing, as she does, a punishment to Tib. for his former hopes of rural simplicity.

59–60 *in Cos ... bands of gold!*: the weavers of Cos produced a diaphanous material like silk. It had erotic and luxurious associations, particularly if, as in this case, it was interwoven with gold threads.

63 *red of Africa*: a scarlet dye made from berries was produced by the Phoenician inhabitants of Carthage in North Africa.

indigo of Tyre: for Tyrian purple, another luxury product, see note to 1.2.77 and cf. 1.9.70.

65–6 *her 'king' ... foreign scaffold*: the reference again is to Tib.'s rival. For the image of the 'kingdom' of love cf. 1.9.80. The implication of 66 is that he was an ex-slave. Slaves on sale from abroad had their feet coated with chalk as a distinguishing mark and were paraded before potential buyers on a temporary wooden scaffold.

74–5 *nuts . . . Nuts fed the ancients*: the Latin for 'nuts' in these two lines is *glans*, referring literally to 'acorns'.

79 *no sad displays outside a door*: the reference is to the shut-out lover: see introductory note to 1.2 and cf. note to 1.5.65.

81 *May Love . . . way of life*: this line is provided by the translator to fill a lacuna in the manuscripts.

82 *in clothes of fur!*: i.e. animal skins, the clothes of primitive men.

84 *a flowing toga?*: the sign of a dandy: see note to 1.6.39–40.

86 *chains and lashes!*: the attributes of slavery: see 1.6.38. Tib. is willing to serve as a chained slave in the country to be near Nemesis.

ELEGY 2.4

The reference to bondage and lack of freedom in the first couplet obviously echoes the final couplet of 2.3 and the two elegies are clearly to be taken together as a pair.

Love imposes slavery to a mistress and endless suffering from which Tib. begs for release (1–12). Poetry cannot help; what use is verse if it cannot provide access to his mistress (13–20)? In such desperation his only option is to turn to sacrilege against Venus to provide the gifts Nemesis demands (21–6). A diatribe against modern luxury, which has given love a bad name (27–38), is followed by a curse on his mercenary mistress; may she lose her wealth and have no one to mourn her death (39–44). By contrast a generous mistress would have an admirer to tend her tomb (45–50). His warnings are useless; in love Nemesis dictates the rules (50–1). For her love he would be prepared to sell his ancestral home and drink down witches' poisons (53–60).

Like 2.3 the elegy reflects a complete reversal of his former ideals. Traces of the earlier Tib. may remain in his criticism of greed and in his praise of the generous mistress, but he has to accept that in a corrupt society he must compromise his ideals to win a mercenary mistress. Everything that had been important to him in his previous life, his devotion to the Muses, his cult of Venus, and his love for the gods of his ancestral home must now be sacrificed to his blind passion for Nemesis.

1–6 *bondage and a mistress*: the opening of the elegy picks up the theme of slavery to love with which the previous poem had ended.

4 *Love never loosens bonds*: here the bonds of servitude, as contrasted with the bonds of marriage which Love is asked to bring for Cornutus in 1.2.

6 *Heartless girl, remove the torch!*: the torch of love is normally wielded by Amor, along with his arrows.

8–9 *a stone . . . the winds*: stones and rocks are regularly used as images of lack of feeling in ancient poetry (cf. 1.1.64).

16 *to sing of wars*: i.e. to write epic.

17–18 *solar routes ... full circle*: the reference is to didactic poetry on astronomical subjects.

19 *Through verse I ask for easy access to my mistress*: a common view of the use of poetry in the Roman elegists: cf. Propertius 1.7.5–12, Ovid, *Amores* 2.1.21–2.

23–6 *grab the sacred emblems ... unholy hands!*: a complete reversal of Tib.'s devotion to Venus in Book 1; contrast 1.2.81–4, 99–100, 1.3.58, 1.4.79, etc.

28 *dye from Tyre*: see note to 1.2.77.

29 *Coan fashion*: see note to 2.3.59–60.

31 *an entrance feels a key*: the theme of the shut-out lover once more: see introductory note to 2.1.

40 *wind and fire*: a variation on the theme of ill-gotten gains turning to water and ash: cf. 1.9.11–12.

50 *and earth be light upon your tranquil ashes*: a variation on the common formula 'may the earth lie lightly over you' found frequently in Greek and Roman funerary inscriptions.

53–4 *my forebears' house ... for-sale sign!*: another example of how his passion for Nemesis has turned on their head Tib.'s former ideals. The importance of ancestral home and household gods (Lares) is a recurrent theme in the first book (cf. 1.3.33–4).

55–6 *Whatever potions ... in drugs*: Circe and Medea were the two most famous witches of antiquity. Circe turned Odysseus' crew into swine; for Medea see note to 1.2.53. Thessaly was the traditional home of witches and their potions. The relevance of witches' brews in this context is their use as love potions.

57–8 *or even ... wild herds*: the reference here is to *hippomanes*, a secretion from the genitalia of mares in heat, famed in the ancient world as an aphrodisiac.

ELEGY 2.5

This is Tib.'s longest and most ambitious elegy. It takes the form of a hymn addressed by the poet to Apollo on the occasion of the induction of Messalla's son, Messallinus, as a member of the priestly college entrusted with the care of the Sibylline books. The priests' duties included the interpretation of the Sibyl's oracles and this allows Tib. to include in the poem the early prophecies revealed to Aeneas about Rome's foundation and more recent oracles concerning the civil wars after the death of Caesar. The elegy begins with Messallinus' induction and ends with a prediction of his future triumph.

Marcus Valerius Messalla Messallinus, whose election to the priesthood is the starting point of the poem, was the eldest son of Tib.'s patron, Messalla. He had a distinguished career, becoming consul in 3 BC and legate in Illyricum in AD 6. He served Tiberius with distinction in a campaign against the

Pannonians and Dalmatians and was rewarded with a triumphal decoration
(*ornamenta triumphalia*) and a place in the procession during Tiberius'
Pannonian triumph in AD 12, four years after his father's death.

At the poem's opening Apollo is asked to appear, dressed as a lyre-player
and crowned with triumphant laurel, to welcome Messallinus to the priest-
hood (1–10). As a prophet himself and as an inspirer of prophets, Apollo
should instruct the new priest in the interpretation of the Sibylline oracles
(11–18). The Sibyl had given Aeneas oracles about the foundation of Rome
after the sack of Troy, when the site of the future city was home to simple
shepherds (19–39). Now begins a direct quotation of that prophecy to Aeneas,
foretelling his settlement in Italy and victories over its native tribes (39–50);
the rise of Rome and its future world domination (51–64). The prophecy is
followed by a short description of the Sibyl (65–6). A number of Sibyls had
prophesied the evil omens that would mark the year of Caesar's assassination
(67–78). Apollo is asked to drown such omens beneath the sea (79–80). As it is,
good omens foretell a year of prosperity for the farmers who will celebrate the
rustic festival of the Palilia (81–104). Tib. ends with a personal prayer that
Apollo should ease the sufferings of his love for Nemesis (105–14) and allow
him, in the company of Messalla, to celebrate in the future a triumph for
Messallinus (115–22).

The arrival of Aeneas in Italy and the early origins of Rome were of course
also the subject of Virgil's epic poem, the *Aeneid*. This was not published in its
final form until 16 BC, three years after Virgil's death. Tib. is known to have
died shortly after Virgil and certainly before 16 BC (see Introduction, p. viii).
Similarities between the two treatments nevertheless suggest that Tib. could
have heard pre-publication recitations of parts of the work. The poem is an
accomplished example of the widening of the range of elegy to include themes
of national importance and, as such, looks forward to such later works as
Ovid's *Fasti* and Propertius' Book 4.

1–2 *Phoebus . . . song and lyre*: the inauguration of Messallinus takes place
   in Apollo's temple. As god of prophecy, Phoebus Apollo was closely
   associated with the Sibyls, whose oracles he inspired. The poet adopts the
   role of an officiating priest at the ceremony, as he had in 2.1.

7–8 *the robe | that's set aside*: gods' statues were dressed in robes only for
   special occasions.

9–10 *when Saturn . . . victor, Jove*: at the end of the Golden Age, Saturn
   was put to flight and replaced by Jove, who inaugurated the Age of Iron
   (see notes to 1.3.35 and 1.3.49).

12–14 *bird . . . lots . . . entrails*: for the three types of divination mentioned—
   augury, sortilege, and haruspicy—see note to 1.8.3–4.

15 *hexameters*: the oracles were given in Greek hexameter verse, the metre
   of Homer's epics and Hesiod's didactic poetry.

20 *Lares*: see note to 1.1.20. Here they refer to the household gods of Aeneas
   in Troy, that were snatched from the hands of the enemy and taken by
   Aeneas to Rome. Cf. Virgil, *Aeneid* 1.378–9: 'I am pious Aeneas, who

carry the Penates [= household gods, cf. 1.3.33 above] snatched from the enemy with me in my fleet.'

23 *timeless city*: in Latin *aeternae ... urbis*; the first extant reference to Rome as 'the eternal city'.

23–4 *Romulus ... Remus*: Romulus was the traditional founder of Rome, some generations after Aeneas' arrival in Italy. His role is kept to a minimum here and all the emphasis is on Aeneas, who set in train the events which led ultimately to Rome's foundation. Line 24 contains a veiled reference to the story that Romulus killed his brother Remus for insulting him by jumping over the walls of his new city.

25 *Palatine*: in Tib.'s day this hill was the site of Augustus' mansion as well as the temple of Apollo.

26 *Jove's hill*: the Capitol, site of the temple of Capitoline Jove.

27–8 *Pan ... Pales*: both rustic deities who had care of the flocks. On Pales, whose festival was on Rome's foundation day, see note to 1.1.36. Like Pales in 1.1.36, Pan was given only non-blood milk offerings, hence 'dripping milk' here.

30 *the tree-god*: probably the native Italian Silvanus (see note to 1.1.14).

33 *Velabrum*: a low-lying region of Rome, sloping down towards the Tiber, which in ancient times had been a navigable marsh.

39 *Flitting Love's brother*: as son of Venus, Aeneas was Cupid's half brother. This and Virgil, *Aeneid* 1.667 are the first extant references to this relationship. The Sibyl's prophecy of the destiny of Rome follows. The Cumaean Sibyl gives a similar prophecy in Virgil, *Aeneid* 6.83–7, but Tib. may perhaps have been influenced here by Tiberinus' prophecy at *Aeneid* 8.36–65.

41 *Laurentum's fields*: land on the left bank of the Tiber, where Aeneas placed his first camp in Italy.

43 *You will be divine ... god of Heaven*: at the end of his life Aeneas turned into a god by the waters of the Numicus (modern Rio Torto) in Latium and was admitted to heaven. Recent archaeological discoveries in the area reveal it to have been a cult centre for the deified Aeneas.

47–8 *Rutulian camps ... Turnus*: Turnus was a chief of the Italian tribe of the Rutuli, who fought Aeneas for Latinus' daughter, Lavinia, previously promised to him as a bride. This is the only account to mention the burning of the Rutulian camp by the Trojans. The death of Turnus comes as the culmination of Virgil's *Aeneid*.

49 *Lavinium's wall*: Aeneas' second and more lasting foundation in Italy after the camp at Laurentum. It was named supposedly after his new wife Lavinia. The modern site of Lavinium is called Pratica di Mare.

50 *King Ascanius' Alba Longa*: Alba Longa was the next Trojan city to be founded in Italy, some thirty years after Lavinium. Its founder was Aeneas' son Ascanius.

51 *Ilia*: a Vestal virgin who was seduced by Mars and gave birth to Romulus and Remus. According to Virgil, *Aeneid* 1.272–4 this took place one hundred years after the foundation of Alba Longa.

55 *Seven Hills!*: an ancient name for the site of Rome.

61 *Troy*: the idea is that Troy will marvel at its rebirth as Rome.

67–70 *Amalthea ... Anio*: the list of Sibyls probably derives from Tib.'s older contemporary, the scholar Varro. He gave a list of ten Sibyls which Tib. here simplifies down to four: the Sibyl of Cumae (Amalthea), a Trojan Sibyl (Herophile from Marpessus beneath Mount Ida in the Troad), a Greek Sibyl (Phoeto, from the Greek island of Samos), and a Roman Sibyl (Albunea, the Sibyl of the Tibur, worshipped on the banks of the Anio). A statue of the Roman Sibyl had been found in the river carrying a book of oracles that had been brought safely to land (see 70).

71 *a comet*: probably the comet reported in 44 BC on the assassination of Caesar. Tib. interprets this not as the ascension to heaven of the deified Caesar (as in Augustan propaganda) but as an evil portent of civil war.

72 *shower land with rocks*: a rain of stones could possibly have resulted from the eruption of Etna in the same year (44 BC).

75 *That shrouded year*: the dimming of the sun's light over a whole year could also be consistent with the after-effects of the volcanic eruption of Etna.

87 *Palilia*: the annual feast of Pales (see note to 1.1.36 and cf. 28 above), held at the end of April, on the anniversary of Rome's foundation, for the purification of flocks and shepherds; hence 'his special feast'.

109–10 *I have lain ... my pain was joy*: two common images for love are present in this couplet: (1) as a wound (from Cupid's bow), (2) as a disease from which the lover has no desire to be cured.

116 *conquered towns*: floats representing towns captured in the campaign would have been part of the triumphal procession (see 1.7.10).

ELEGY 2.6

The reference to 'slamming doors' (12) reveals this poem, somewhat belatedly, as a shut-out lover's song in the same tradition as 1.2 and 1.5. The monologue is to be imagined as a final desperate entreaty to the unresponsive Nemesis spoken outside her locked door.

Macer is going to war. Will Love accompany him? (1–6). If Love spares soldiers I too will take up arms and say goodbye to girls (7–10). This is just empty bravado sent flying by my mistress's slammed door. I cannot keep away from her (11–14). Would that Love's weapons could be destroyed for driving me to distraction in this way (14–18). Suicide would have ended my pain, had I not been encouraged by Hope, who promises Nemesis will look on me with favour. She, however, says no. Cruel girl, do not fight against a goddess

(19–28). Have pity, for your dead sister's sake, at whose grave I pray in supplication. Do not be harsh to me or you will be haunted by her blood-stained ghost (29–40). I have no wish to renew my mistress's distress. It is not Nemesis but her bawd who keeps me locked outside, while I die of frustration and jealousy. Bawd, I curse you, may your future life be full of fear (41–54).

The juxtaposition of love and war and the theme of Hope link the elegy to the first poem of the first book and thus provide a satisfactory ring structure for the whole collection.

1 *Macer*: the identity of the addressee is uncertain. Two poets are possible candidates: (1) Aemilius Macer, from Verona, a friend of Virgil and Ovid and author of poems on birds, beasts, and medicine, who died in Asia Minor in 16 BC, possibly on the campaign mentioned here; (2) Pompeius Macer, a friend of Ovid, who wrote epic poetry in which love played a significant role. There is no proof that either of these is meant and the name could simply be a pseudonym appropriate to a lover, with its suggestion of 'leanness' (*macer* = 'thin', 'lean') often seen as a charac-teristic of lovers in elegy.

5 *boy*: refers to Love (Amor, Cupid).

6 *rebel*: the Latin *erronem* may refer either to a runaway slave, or, as is more likely here, a deserting soldier. The image again is that of love as military service with Cupid as a general.

12 *slamming doors*: fix the poem's context as a shut-out lover's lament.

16 *darts ... arrows ... torches*: the conventional weapons of Cupid.

19–27 *Hope ... Nemesis*: the prayer to personified Hope here picks up the mention of Hope in 1.1.9–10 and thus provides an element of ring-structure to the two books. Hope had been deified by the Greeks and possessed a temple in Rome from the earliest times. There was a traditional antithesis between Hope and Nemesis in Greek poetry and religion, which gives added point to 27 here: Hope promises, but Nemesis says no.

29 *your sister's doll-like bones*: the use by Tib. of an appeal to Nemesis' dead sister's bones and the threat that her ghost will haunt her if she remains unresponsive (l. 40) emphasizes Tib.'s desperation.

39–40 *bloodspattered ... upstairs window*: the ghosts of the dead were thought to retain their appearance at the moment of death (see note to 1.10.40). The urban poor of Rome lived in multi-storey tenements. Fatal falls from such high places are sometimes recalled on funerary inscriptions (see F. Buecheler and E. Lommatzsch (eds.), *Carmina Latina Epigraphica* (Leipzig, 1895–1926), 462, 1901).

44 *Her madam's mean*: the shifting of the blame from the mistress onto a wicked 'madam' or 'bawd' is a common tactic of the shut-out lover (see 1.5.47ff.).

45 *Phryne*: a common name for prostitutes in Greek real life and literature. Its meaning in Greek is 'toad'.

TEXTUAL NOTES

The present text departs from the Ambrosian manuscript (see Note on the Text) in the following instances:[1]

Line reference	Ambrosian manuscript	This edition
1.1.14	agricolae	agricolam
1.1.19	felices	felicis
1.1.24	clamat	clamet
1.1.25	non possum	iam possim
1.1.29	ludentes	bidentem
1.1.37	et	neu
1.1.44	scilicet	si licet
1.1.49	si	sit
1.1.54	exiles	hostiles
1.1.59	et	te
1.1.60	et	te
1.1.63	dura	duro
1.1.64	iuncta	uincta
1.1.73	posses	postes
1.2.23	decet	docet
1.2.42	rapido	rabido (excerpta Puccii)
1.2.60	ipse	ille
1.2.67	possit	posset
1.2.71	contextus	contectus
1.2.80	posset	possit
1.2.81	magni	magnae
1.2.84	diripuisse	deripuisse
1.2.89	laetus	lentus (Broukhusius)
1.2.90	non unus	et iratus
1.3.4	modo nigra	precor atra
1.3.9	cum	quam (Dousa pater)
1.3.12	triuiis	trinis (Broukhusius)
1.3.14	cum	quin (Aldine 1502)
1.3.17	dant	aut
1.3.18	Saturni	Saturniue (anon in 16th cent.)
1.3.21	neu	ne
1.3.22	sciat	sciet (Döring)
1.3.25	deum	dum
1.3.38	ueteris	uentis
1.3.50	reperte	repente

[1] If the reading used in this edition is not found in a later manuscript the name of the scholar who is believed first to have conjectured it is given in brackets after the reading.

Line reference	Ambrosian manuscript	This edition
1.3.59	passuque	passimque
1.3.86	colo	colu
1.3.91	nunc	tunc
1.4.8	sit	sic
1.4.28	remeatque	remeatue
1.4.29	te perdit	deperdit
1.4.36	illam	ullam
1.4.40	credas	cedas
1.4.44	amiciat	admittat
1.4.44	imbrifer	nubifer
1.4.53	mihi	tibi
1.4.53	cum	tunc
1.4.54	tamen apta	tibi rapta (Santen)
1.4.59	iam	at
1.4.62	ne	nec
1.4.63	est (omitted)	est
1.4.71	ipsa	illa (Heyne)
1.4.72	flentibus	fletibus
1.4.80	diducat	deducat
1.4.81	heheu	eheu
1.5.1	dissidium	discidium
1.5.2	sortis	fortis
1.5.3	turbo	turben
1.5.6	post haec	posthac
1.5.7	parce	per te
1.5.16	uoca nouem creme	uota nouem Triuiae
1.5.28	segete et spicas	segete spicas
1.5.30	adiuuet	at iuuet
1.5.42	mea	meam (Nodell)
1.5.45	Nereis quae	Nereis
1.5.55	urbes	urbem (Castiglioni)
1.5.61	tibi praesto	semper tibi (Muretus)
1.5.67	iuncta	uicta
1.5.69	furta	fata
1.5.74	ipse	usque
1.5.76	nam	nat
1.6.11	nunc	tunc
1.6.18	lasso	laxo
1.6.40	effluit	et fluit
1.6.42	stet procul ante	transeat ille (Lee)
1.6.45	mota	motu
1.6.46	non et amans	non amens
1.6.47	uiolata	uiolenta
1.6.52	didicisse	tetigisse (Achilles Statius)
1.6.67	uicta	uitta

Line reference	*Ambrosian manuscript*	*This edition*
1.6.70	possum	possim
1.6.71	putat ductor	putet ducarque
1.6.72	proprias proripiorque	pronas proripiarque
1.6.84	quod	quam
1.7.4	Atax	Atur (Scaliger)
1.7.6	uinctos	euinctos
1.7.9	tua belli	Tarbella (Scaliger)
1.7.12	Carnoti	Carnutis
1.7.13	at	an
1.7.16	arat	alat
1.7.40	tristitiae	laetitiae (Muretus)
1.7.42	cuspide	conpede
1.7.49	centum ludos	Genium ludis (Markland)
1.7.54	mella	melle
1.7.57	ne	nec
1.7.57	quae	quem
1.7.61	canit	canat
1.7.57	a (omitted)	a
1.8.1	celare	celari
1.8.2	ferat	ferant
1.8.2	leuia	lenia
1.8.11	comas	genas
1.8.29	ne	nec
1.8.49	seu	neu
1.8.51	sentita	sontica
1.8.52	luteo	luto
1.8.57	leuis	lenis
1.8.59	quamuis	quauis (Kraffert)
1.8.61	possunt	prosunt
1.8.64	euigilanda	uigilanda (Francken)
1.8.77	at	et (P. Burmann II)
1.9.9	petituros	petituras
1.9.19	o uiciis	diuitiis
1.9.23	celanti fas	celandi spes
1.9.24	sit	scit
1.9.24	uetet	uetat
1.9.25	leue	saepe (Muretus)
1.9.31	tibi	te
1.9.35	eriperet	eriperes
1.9.36	puras	pronas (Heyne)
1.9.40	sit	sic
1.9.40	sed	sit
1.9.44	sed	et
1.9.44	clausos	clausas
1.9.68	pectore	pectere

Line reference	Ambrosian manuscript	This edition
1.9.69	ista	istane (Postgate)
1.9.73	haec	nec
1.9.75	hunc	huic
1.9.81	dum	tunc
1.10.8	ciphus	scyphus
1.10.18	ueteres	ueteris
1.10.21	uua	uuam
1.10.23	ipsa`	ipse
1.10.32	aduerso	aduersos
1.10.38	puppis	turpis
1.10.51	uidens uomer	bidens uomerque
1.10.51	uiderit	nitent (Guyet)
1.10.53	elutoque	e lucoque
1.10.53	ipso	ipse
1.10.62	diripit	deripit
1.10.63	perscindere	rescindere
1.10.70	praefluat	perfluat
2.1.1	ualeat	faueat (Scaliger)
2.1.9	sunt	sint
2.1.23	satiri	saturi
2.1.34	ades	auis (Scaliger)
2.1.38	grande famen	glande famem
2.1.42	suppotuisse	supposuisse
2.1.45	antea	aurea
2.1.49	ingerat	ingerit
2.1.50	et	ut
2.1.54	duceret	diceret
2.1.58	yrcus hauxerat hyrcus oues	paruas auxerat hircus opes (Postgate)
2.1.65	Mineruam	Mineruae
2.1.66	appulso	a pulso (Muretus)
2.1.73	opus	opes
2.1.74	limem	limen
2.1.88	thoro	choro
2.1.89	fuluis	furuis
2.2.7	distillent	destillent
2.2.15	undis	Indis
2.2.19	uinculaque	uincula quae
2.3.11	armenti	Admeti
2.3.18	mixtus	mixtis (Muretus)
2.3.47	obsistere	obsidere
2.3.48	et	ut
2.3.49	tumulti	tumultu
2.3.53	tibi	mihi
2.3.59	gerit	gerat

Line reference	*Ambrosian manuscript*	*This edition*
2.3.65	que	quem
2.3.66	bipsatos	gypsatos
2.3.67	seges Memesis qui abducit	Ceres, Nemesim quae abducis (Heinsius)
2.3.74	et (omitted)	et
2.3.84	iuuet	iuuat
2.4.2	pater ue	paterna
2.4.4	remittet	remittit
2.4.5	quid	nil (Heinsius)
2.4.10	uasti (omitted)	uasti
2.4.12	nam	nunc
2.4.17	equalis	et qualis
2.4.17	urbem	orbem
2.4.33	incerta	uicta
2.4.36	ipse	ille
2.4.38	hic	nunc (Broukhusius)
2.4.40	portas	partas
2.4.43	seu	heu (Camps)
2.4.44	obsequias	exsequias
2.4.55	quidquam	quidquid
2.4.59	non	modo
2.5.4	meas	mea (Lachmann)
2.5.11	debitus	deditus
2.5.18	quos	quid
2.5.20	captos	raptos
2.5.34	pulla	pulsa
2.5.35	illaque	illa saepe
2.5.35	ditis	diti (Muretus)
2.5.47	rutilis	Rutulis
2.5.49	castris	castrum
2.5.52	longam . . . uiam	longa . . . uia
2.5.64	noscar	uescar
2.5.68	Phoebo	Phyto (Huschke)
2.5.68	grata	Graia (Lachmann)
2.5.69	quodque Albana sacras Tiberis	quasque Aniena sacras Tiburs
2.5.70	portarit . . . perlueritque	portarat . . . pertuleratque (Postgate)
2.5.72	et	ut
2.5.72	deplueritque	deplueretque
2.5.76	amnis	annus
2.5.79	fuerant	fuerunt
2.5.81	ut	et
2.5.82	sacer	satur (Cornelissen)
2.5.92	compressis	comprensis

Line reference	Ambrosian manuscript	This edition
2.5.94	puro	puero
2.5.95	operta	operata
2.5.99	exstruat	exstruet
2.5.109	taceo	iaceo
2.5.116	ferent	feret
2.5.122	perpetua	perpetuo
2.6.16	scilicet	si licet
2.6.32	ferant	feram
2.6.45	Phirne	Phryne
2.6.46	tuncque	itque
2.6.47	diro	duro

The Oxford World's Classics Website

www.worldsclassics.co.uk

- Browse the full range of Oxford World's Classics online

- Sign up for our monthly e-alert to receive information on new titles

- Read extracts from the Introductions

- Listen to our editors and translators talk about the world's greatest literature with our Oxford World's Classics audio guides

- Join the conversation, follow us on Twitter at OWC_Oxford

- Teachers and lecturers can order inspection copies quickly and simply via our website

www.worldsclassics.co.uk

American Literature

British and Irish Literature

Children's Literature

Classics and Ancient Literature

Colonial Literature

Eastern Literature

European Literature

Gothic Literature

History

Medieval Literature

Oxford English Drama

Poetry

Philosophy

Politics

Religion

The Oxford Shakespeare

A complete list of Oxford World's Classics, including Authors in Context, Oxford English Drama, and the Oxford Shakespeare, is available in the UK from the Marketing Services Department, Oxford University Press, Great Clarendon Street, Oxford OX2 6DP, or visit the website at www.oup.com/uk/worldsclassics.

In the USA, visit www.oup.com/us/owc for a complete title list.

Oxford World's Classics are available from all good bookshops. In case of difficulty, customers in the UK should contact Oxford University Press Bookshop, 116 High Street, Oxford OX1 4BR.

HORACE	The Complete Odes and Epodes
JUVENAL	The Satires
LIVY	The Dawn of the Roman Empire
	Hannibal's War
	The Rise of Rome
MARCUS AURELIUS	The Meditations
OVID	The Love Poems
	Metamorphoses
PETRONIUS	The Satyricon
PLATO	Defence of Socrates, Euthyphro, and Crito
	Gorgias
	Meno and Other Dialogues
	Phaedo
	Republic
	Selected Myths
	Symposium
PLAUTUS	Four Comedies
PLUTARCH	Greek Lives
	Roman Lives
	Selected Essays and Dialogues
PROPERTIUS	The Poems
SOPHOCLES	Antigone, Oedipus the King, and Electra
STATIUS	Thebaid
SUETONIUS	Lives of the Caesars
TACITUS	Agricola and Germany
	The Histories
VIRGIL	The Aeneid
	The Eclogues and Georgics
XENOPHON	The Expedition of Cyrus

A SELECTION OF   **OXFORD WORLD'S CLASSICS**

	Travel Writing 1700–1830
	Women's Writing 1778–1838
WILLIAM BECKFORD	**Vathek**
JAMES BOSWELL	**Life of Johnson**
FRANCES BURNEY	**Camilla**
	Cecilia
	Evelina
	The Wanderer
LORD CHESTERFIELD	**Lord Chesterfield's Letters**
JOHN CLELAND	**Memoirs of a Woman of Pleasure**
DANIEL DEFOE	**A Journal of the Plague Year**
	Moll Flanders
	Robinson Crusoe
	Roxana
HENRY FIELDING	**Jonathan Wild**
	Joseph Andrews and Shamela
	Tom Jones
WILLIAM GODWIN	**Caleb Williams**
OLIVER GOLDSMITH	**The Vicar of Wakefield**
MARY HAYS	**Memoirs of Emma Courtney**
ELIZABETH INCHBALD	**A Simple Story**
SAMUEL JOHNSON	**The History of Rasselas**
	The Major Works
CHARLOTTE LENNOX	**The Female Quixote**
MATTHEW LEWIS	**Journal of a West India Proprietor**
	The Monk
HENRY MACKENZIE	**The Man of Feeling**

A SELECTION OF   OXFORD WORLD'S CLASSICS